Goandria: The Schism

R. Michael

To my amazing wife.

Map of Goandria

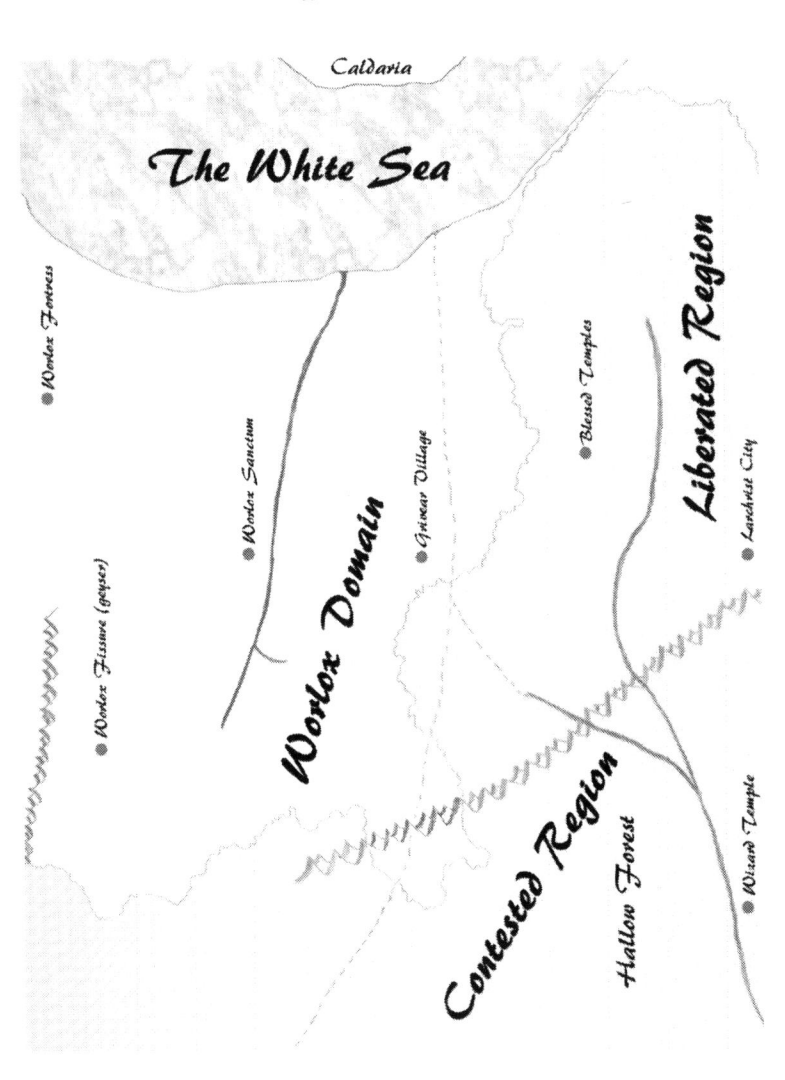

Caldaria

The White Sea

Worlox Fortress

Worlox Sanctum

Worlox Fissure (geyser)

Worlox Domain

Grivear Village

Blessed Temples

Liberated Region

Larchrist City

Contested Region

Hallow Forest

Wizard Temple

Table of Contents

Part I

Chapter 1 1

Chapter 2 7

Chapter 3 17

Chapter 4 28

Part II

Chapter 1 41

Chapter 2 52

Chapter 3 60

Chapter 4 70

Chapter 5 80

Chapter 6 88

Chapter 7 95

Part III

Chapter 1 107

Chapter 2 113

Chapter 3 120

Chapter 4 127

Chapter 5 134

Chapter 6 146

Chapter 7 157

Chapter 8 164

Chapter 9 172

Chapter 10 178

Epilogue 184

Goandria: The Schism

Part I

Chapter 1

Gray and black clouds marched across the once-blue sky. The wind stripped many of the trees of their orange and red foliage. Before long, the darkened sky flashed with bolts of lighting, and thunder rolled in the distance like ominous war drums. A sea of hardwood trees swayed as far as the eye could see in every direction, but in the center of a clearing rose two towers.

The towers were tall, and their walls blazed white, even amongst the coming darkness. The polished stone flawlessly highlighted the craftsmanship of their architect. Each tower looked as if it was carved out of a single piece of stone. Compounding this illusion, no windows were set in the stonework, for their inhabitants did not require any such hindrances to the structures' beauty. They were pyramidal in shape, but elongated so they appeared stretched upward. They were joined by a bridge near the top of the towers which was accented by a series of flying buttresses. Statues of warriors lined the outside of the structures as well as several walkways that merged into a single road that was the only way in or out of the towers.

Along the stone road, a chocolate-brown horse bore its blue-cloaked rider. Two score similarly-clad individuals came out to greet the rider. The horseman threw back his hood revealing a pronounced jaw and brow bone, long, brown hair, and a short beard that covered his face and neck. He stood taller than his peers, a little over six-feet tall, and his entire frame was reinforced by bulging muscles. Beneath his cloak, he wore a steel breastplate with chainmail sleeves, and a bronze-hilted, hand-and-a-half sword hung at his belt.

"Welcome general," a woman greeted the horseman. "What news do you bring?"

"Come now, haven't we known each other long enough to drop such formalities, Evera?" the man smirked.

"Well you know," Evera giggled, "since you have become the leader of the military and all, I don't know."

"Oh come now, you have just as important a position documenting battles while sitting at a desk."

"Same old Kai. Not a humble bone in your body."

"If you two are done, we have a lot to discuss," another cut in. Beneath his blue cloak sat a white-bearded, wrinkled face. His eyes were brown and steely as they looked unblinkingly at the general.

"Of course. My apologies Magister."

"Have you managed to drive the worlox any further north?" asked the Magister.

"Only minimally, and at great cost. We lost hundreds of wizards in the campaign to drive the demons out of Goandria. Their strength seems to be wavering, but it is still impossible to tell just how much strength they have remaining. Their underground dwellings are labyrinthine and go on for miles and miles."

"Lorkai, I think I have a new assignment for you…"

"I'm listening, but first there is something else that I wanted to bring up to you," Lorkai interrupted. "Several of our brother and sisters have been captured by the enemy. I was hoping for permission to send a battalion to go rescue them."

"A whole battalion? That is more than I feel comfortable committing to such a campaign when we may have found a way to return the worlox back to the spiritual realm. But we will need someone with your talents to head northward into the heart of their domain and see if we can open the portal," the Magister replied.

Lorkai's face contorted. "I fail to see the problem. Even if only one wizard was captured, it would be worth the effort for a rescue."

"Yes, but we are at war, and in war, sacrifices must be made. Those men and women knew what they signed up for when they set out for battle."

"But…"

The Magister raised his hand. "Your concerns will be taken into consideration my friend. For now we must celebrate, for our champion has finally returned home, and we are one step closer to victory."

Lorkai and Evera followed behind the Magister and their fellow wizards as they were led to the dining hall. "He never changes, does he?" Evera whispered with a smile.

"No, stubborn as a mule that man is. It must be nice to always be right."

"It's so nice to see you again. So how are you doing really?"

"I definitely missed my little buddy out on the front lines. There were so many times I wished you were there to help keep me sane."

"I missed you too. Sometimes I wished I was out there fighting with you. It can get… stuffy… in here after a while," Evera said, tilting her head towards the Magister.

"At least here you get warm meals and a real bed. Evera, you do not want to see what I see."

"And at least you get a feast in your honor," Evera winked.

"I definitely cannot complain about that."

The general was led into the eastern tower, even though he had travelled the hallways dozens of times before. Along every corridor, wizards and civilians alike lined up to greet Lorkai, shaking his hand as he walked by. Several women embraced him exclaiming, "Praise Voshnore for you and your victories!"

"Looks like I still got it," he said, nudging Evera.

"Yes, a swollen head…"

After a long white hallway, the Magister swung open two oak doors that were several inches thick, holding his hand out to let Lorkai be the first to pass through. Upon entering the tapestry-laden room, the smell of freshly-roasted meats and simmered vegetables slammed his nostrils. About a hundred wizards were already in the dining hall and offered a standing applause upon seeing their guest of honor.

"Please sit at the head table in the back. We hope that you will find everything to your liking, general," announced the Magister. This was followed by another round of applause.

Once Lorkai took his place, he raised his hands. Suddenly all were silent, their eyes fixed on him. "Gentlemen, ladies, fellow wizards, it has been our sacred duty to protect Goandria since Voshnore blessed the first of our kind.

"Then generations ago, the worlox came and quickly defeated all who stood in their destructive path. All save the wizards, whose weapons were the only ones who could send those creatures back to the land they came from. We have been fighting so long and so hard, with no real victories to speak of, until these last few years when we have finally been able to push the worlox further northward. My friends, this is just the beginning! I will keep pushing forward, I will not stop, and I will save you all from the worlox demons that infest our lands!"

A series of cheers erupted from the crowd. Some began chanting the general's name while others simply sat back down to tend to their food. Evera took her place next to her friend, and together they sat down. Beside her was a middle-aged man with graying brown hair who leaned forward and inclined his head slightly. "So general, since you have at last returned, what are your plans now?"

"To sleep in a bed; heck I would even take the floor with a pillow at this point." Lorkai smirked.

"I can imagine. It has been some time since I fought in the wars myself. Back then we had no sanctuaries such as this; the worlox were everywhere."

"I will see to it that we never return to such times. We will be free, and I will not let them return to this land."

"And so far you have kept that promise. I cannot thank you enough for what you have done, Lorkai."

"It's a process. Soon I will secure total victory."

"Speaking of, the Magister mentioned he had a new assignment, that he and the council have found a way to reopen the portal to the spiritual realm and return the demons to their own realm."

Lorkai leaned forward and glanced around the room for a few seconds. "Yes, he mentioned something about it, but he was quiet about the details. To me, it seems too good to be true. What do you know about this supposed miracle plan, Romma?"

Romma let out a prolonged sigh, "Not much, just that it is being peddled as the means to end the war. I do know the Magister and the council have been working tirelessly behind closed doors. Anything is possible I suppose."

"That's what concerns me."

Chapter 2

Red, blue, and green lightning flashed. Countless bodies lay as far as the eye could see. Black and gray armored soldiers with flaming eyes moved in, their hands holding long, yet narrow, black swords. He looked around frantically. As far as he could see, there were no wizards left standing. He was alone. Then he looked upward. Across the sky streaked a blue fire mass that transformed into a canine-like creature. For a moment, the beast of blue fire hovered over him. "I am the future," it whispered, and then dissipated. Suddenly, a surge of energy erupted throughout his entire body. His skin and hair became the color of charcoal, and electricity flowed through his veins. With a flick of his wrist, the soldiers all evaporated to ash.

Lorkai's eyes snapped open as he quickly sat up, throwing his blankets aside. His sheets were soaked, and beads of sweat covered his entire body. His heart pounded as he took in several deep breaths, but still it beat harder and harder as the memories of the dream came back to him. "What does it all mean?" he uttered to himself. He eyed the robe hanging across the room and walked over, draping it around himself. Silently, Lorkai closed the door behind him. He continued down a hallway for a dozen paces and then turned right and walked down another corridor until he reached the very end.

Lorkai knocked on an oaken door. He waited a few minutes, but there was no answer. He let out a short sigh and knocked again. A couple minutes passed again. He was just about ready to turn back when door creaked open, revealing Evera's long, slender face and golden locks.

"Kai?" she yawned, rubbing her left eye.

"I'm sorry. I know it's late. I just…" he trailed off.

"Hey, I'm here. What do you need?"

"You mind if I come in? I really don't want to be alone right now."

"Of course." she motioned him inside.

Lorkai took a seat on the small bed. "I just got back, and I'm already waking you in the middle of the night because of a stupid dream."

"Hey, I missed you, and I'm glad to be here for you. Besides, this is one of the only times we can actually talk freely. So what's up? You had a bad dream?"

"Well, more than that. We have both seen a lot, and I'm sure bad dreams aren't things you are unfamiliar with. I have them almost nightly, but this one, I felt like I was right there. It felt *real*, like I was right there."

"Tell me about it."

"I was on a battlefield. Worlox infantry as far as the eye could see. All the wizards were killed except me. The sky was dark but filled with different colored lightning. There was an oppressive sense of doom looming over me. I felt powerless as I have never felt before, and then I saw it. A wolf spirit, or something like it, came down and took hold of me. I felt an anger surge through me, like pure rage. I was able to wield a magic more powerful than what we wizards are used to, and I was able to obliterate my enemies. It was utter power. None could withstand me, but this all came at a great cost. My heart withered, and I became blackened inside and out, as black as night, and I cared for no one and nothing save for more power. Before I awoke, I heard the wolf say, 'I am your future.' It was just too real. It didn't feel like a regular dream. What does this all mean?"

Evera's brow furrowed, and she placed a hand on Lorkai's knee. "I don't know. Maybe it was nothing more than it was, a dream. Maybe Voshnore sent you a vision."

"What if this was a vision? What if there is some other source of our power aside from Voshnore?"

"You know our magic only exists as a gift from him so that we can protect Goandria. Nothing more."

"But that is exactly what we are doing right now, and we have accomplished precious little."

"Even if such a power does exist, and this was not just a simple nightmare, it sounds to me like this power would come at a terrible price. Is that worth it to you?"

Lorkai smiled. "Of course not."

"You've got to ask yourself, does it really matter whether this was just a dream or something else? You would never choose to defeat the worlox at such a high cost. The future is not predetermined, and we are not just pieces in a board game. We determine the future, Lorkai. Never forget that."

"You keep me sane, Evera. Did I ever tell you that?" Lorkai smiled.

"Many, many times, but I can never hear it enough." She elbowed him, smiling back.

"Something must have happened, though," Lorkai murmured. "The worlox are being pushed back far easier than they ever have been. They are planning something, perhaps luring us in, making sure we become overconfident, so they can crush us. Fewer worlox foot soldiers meet us on the battlefield. No one has seen one of their overlords in years, and we still do not know what sort of leadership structure they have. We have been fighting those demons for generations, and we still know precious little about them. Now all of a sudden, they appear weak when they have had the advantage for so long? I do not buy it. And I am still very uncomfortable with this new plan to vanquish the worlox. It just seems awfully convenient to me that such a solution would present itself at this point."

"Or maybe you are just overthinking this?"

"I am a general. It is my job to examine all outcomes and possibilities as I see them."

"And for all that, things still surprise us in battle," Evera countered.

"Yes, you are right, like always," Lorkai sighed. "We never really got a chance for you to tell me how you were doing while I was away."

"Oh, you mean you care that I study scrolls all day?" Evera smirked.

"Okay, okay, I deserved that. I do care. How have you been since you retired from battle? Are you feeling any better?"

"My left arm still throbs, and the muscles like to freeze up on me occasionally, but I'm doing much better. I have had a hard time fitting in. I'm not really good at being a scholar. The Magister and the council are as legalistic as always, but they seem to be getting worse lately. Before your return, the atmosphere seemed tense here. It's like there is some big secret, and I'm the only one out of the loop."

"You took quite a blast from the worlox, it's amazing you are in as good of shape as you are. There was a while there I was afraid we were going to lose you. And if there is some secret floating around I have yet to hear it as well, and I am leading our armies."

"I can't wait to return to the battlefield. At least things there make sense. At least there I do not have bureaucracy around every corner. I don't know. Maybe I am just reading into things, or being within these walls is making me feel like a caged animal, but at the very least I feel a shift. Like something is going on within our order."

Lorkai took her hand. "I will defeat them, Evera. Whether this new plan of the Magister's will work or not, I will be the one to destroy the worlox. I can feel it. I will protect you and everyone else. I couldn't stand to see you get hurt again, so do not be so quick to wish yourself back into their line of fire."

"I don't fear them. They had a lucky shot."

"What if they get another 'lucky shot'?"

"Haven't I proven that I can take care of myself, Kai?"

"You sure have, but I'm tired of losing the people I care about. Our race is being hunted like animals, few take up arms against the worlox, and even fewer have the right weapons to fight them. Rumors say that some even joined the worlox. The cowardly englifs fled to their island. It's all on me now."

"No, no, it's not. You need to let others help you. You need to let me help you."

"You can help me by staying alive, unlike Largth, Ilma, Ulnon…the list goes on and on."

"Everyone has lost much. The world was turned upside-down so long ago few remember how it was when the worlox didn't rule us, when they didn't herd us like cattle and put people in sanctioned territories."

"Well, tomorrow I will talk to the Magister and try to get some more information about his plans."

"Maybe see what you can do about getting me out of here, too?"

Lorkai shook his head slightly. "You don't give up do you? One thing, though, is that it is late, and I should let you get some sleep." Lorkai stood up and stepped through the doorway. "Thank you for listening," he said as he shut the door behind him.

Sun streamed through the stone face of the temple's walls. Lorkai stopped for a moment. The sprawling evergreen forest before him suddenly stole his attention. The walls of this particular hallway were a series of ten foot squares that became translucent when as he neared them. The wizard touched the stone. Its transparency distorted around the edges, like looking through the bottom of a bottle, making some of the trees appear fuzzy or elongated. This viewing area was one of the many wonders of the wizard temples. *I can only imagine what other secrets you are keeping from us. You have become so cryptic and secretive while you send us soldiers out to do your dirty work, to keep you safe. Your secrets, Magister, will be your undoing. You wield such power, and yet you sit in a tower*, Lorkai thought as his fingertips gingerly streaked across the polished stone.

A few minutes passed. Lorkai's stare remained on the woodland that spanned miles. Leaves ranging from the size of a man's palm to less than a fingernail fluttered in the northerly wind. Eastward was the only region of the forest that was traveled regularly. A few roads had been carved through the primitive forest which hadn't quite made it west of the Temple yet. It was also rumored that westward, the violet and gold leaves attracted spirits. Many who ventured that direction had not been heard from again, but such things were no more than wives' tales to the wizard. As he looked over the expanse of the trees, his jaw clenched and expression hardened. "I have a feeling someday you will get what's coming to you," he mumbled. The wizard continued on his way; along several corridors and up five flights of stairs before, at last, he came to the topmost level of the eastern tower. The hexagonal room's roof tapered to a point and the royal blue walls were decorated with various swords, bows and spears.

"Welcome, Lorkai," the Magister's voice echoed. He and about two-dozen other aged wizards sat around a glossy, black hexagonal table that nearly filled the room.

"Thank you Magister."

"Please take a seat. We have much to discuss." The Magister motioned to one of the empty chairs.

"Indeed we do, Magister, but I'm not one for long debates and discussions, and to be honest, I would like to just cut to the chase. We have had some decisive victories against the worlox, but nothing that will turn the tide completely in our favor. In response to this, you have sent me less troops, and you blindside me with information that you want me to go into the heart of their realm to help you activate some mystical doomsday weapon that will send them all back to where they came from. Forgive me Magister, councilmen, but this all seems very convenient, and I am having a hard time believing any of your plans will work."

"Anything else you would like to…get off your chest?" A councilman with long red hair and a short beard fingered a ring around his index finger.

"I bet you have been holding that in for quite some time, Lorkai," said the Magister.

"You'd better believe it. I'm out there every day fighting to make this world better so we do not have to endure the worlox rule for yet another generation, and you old cronies sit around talking amongst one another. You have done very little to aid our efforts, and it's time someone called you out on it."

"Watch it, boy. We are still your superiors," reprimanded the Magister.

"See, that's just it. You all think you are superior."

"SILENCE!" the Magister yelled out. A few moments of utter quiet ensued before he spoke again. "We have our reasons for the secrets we keep. The possibility of creating a portal has been in the works for a year now. We have been experimenting with bending our powers in such a way that we can focus all of our energy on opening a gateway into the spiritual realm. The idea is that since Voshnore gave us our magic with a connection to the spiritual world, we can have some sort of limited access if enough energy is directed to it. However, one of exceptional skill is required to be a conduit for the portal, and that is where you come in Lorkai."

Lorkai's jaw was tight and his eyes bore silently into the Magister. "Meaning?" he asked.

"You have always demonstrated talents other wizards do not have: your extreme prowess in battle, your manipulation of wizard lightning to strike multiple targets at once, and you do not need to use your sword to focus the energy of your power like most wizards. This is just to name a few examples of why you are the general of our armies and why you are perfect for this job," said the Magister.

"So what exactly does this mission look like? I still haven't been told what I'm doing when I get up there."

"You will know when the time is right. For now this is all the information we can give you," replied the Magister.

"And you are saying I'm the only one who can carry your plans out?" Lorkai asked.

"Most certainly not the only one, but the preferred one. Isn't it time we put an end to this war and bring peace to Goandria?"

"What of our prisoners they are detaining? You still expect me to just forget about them? I will not do this mission unless you grant me what I need to free them. And I do not like this plan of yours any better. I have a feeling it is a one-way mission, or that you haven't got a clue as to how everything will work out. While I am suspicious of how sparse the worlox resistance has been of late, at least I know where I stand with military tactics.

I ask instead of using some experimental mystical weapon that *might* work, I suggest you commit more wizards from this temple and the Blessed Temples to the front lines."

The councilmen murmured amongst themselves for a moment, but the Magister motioned for silence. He loosed a short sigh. "We will have to discuss your request and get back to you in a couple days. You ask much, but, I will admit, it is not entirely unreasonable. After spending some time thinking about what you said yesterday, I agree that it would be ideal to bring your soldiers back home. However, we are at war, and there are practicalities to consider."

Lorkai clenched his jaw again. "If that is your decision, so be it," he said between his teeth.

As the meeting progressed, Lorkai's chin rested upon his left palm, and he stared off toward the ceiling. *Look at them, the fools. They sit here offering sanctimonious platitudes to end the war. What do they know of such things? Have any of these cronies left these walls for any other reason than to travel to another temple? Is there any point in me being here anymore? I said all I needed to say. I think it is time to go,* he thought as he suddenly stood up and proceeded to walk out.

The Magister furrowed his brow and raised his palms upward, "Lorkai, do you have somewhere else to be?"

"Indeed I do, anywhere I can be away from such sniveling, self-righteous hypocrites," Lorkai's voice boomed as he closed the doors of the chamber behind him.

Chapter 3

The sun's rays just started to peek up, turning the sky into a painting with strokes of violet, deep red, and orange. Lorkai stroked his chin as he gazed out the viewing area in his room. The wizard's eyes were bloodshot, and bags hung under his eyelids, yet his pulse raced and his fingers drummed on the arm of the chair in which he sat. He watched, biding his time as the sun made its slow ascent over the eastern horizon. When at last the orb was fully visible, Lorkai quickly stood up and hastened to Evera's room. When she answered, Lorkai quickly ducked inside. "I need you to come with me. Take only what is necessary. We will be traveling light."

"Hey, Kai, what are you doing?"

"There is no time. Please, Evera, hurry!"

"I'm going to need a little more to go on."

"We are going to rescue the prisoners from my unit. The Magister and the council are dragging their feet, and the longer we wait, the less likely it is that they are still alive."

"So you just naturally assumed that I would willingly rebel against the Magister and his wishes?" she asked, cocking her head to one side.

"Well I, uhh…"

Evera chuckled. "Of course I'm in, Kai." She smiled. "But we can't just go alone."

"I'm thinking Emir and Lauren will join us, perhaps more. If the truth were known, more people are probably loyal to me than to the Magister."

"More importantly than feeding your ego, what is your plan? Ambush everyone you mentioned like you did me?"

Lorkai exhaled deeply. "I don't know. I wish it could be that easy, but to rebel against the wishes of the Magister may take some convincing."

"I thought you were relying on their complete loyalty to you." Evera smirked.

"Oh, I am, but that is just part of it. We need something that will shake their faith in the Magister. We need to show that he and the council are weak."

"Didn't you want to leave soon?" Evera asked.

"Hmm, you are right. We need to get going if there is to be any chance of saving them."

"Now you are suggesting we go alone? But that would be suicide!"

"What other option do we have?"

"We could be patient, Lorkai. You just said we will need other wizards to help us, and suddenly you want to just jump in alone. Which is it?"

"I don't know, Evera! Either way has its risks, but the more I talk about it, the more I have come to believe that any sort of delay puts their lives in greater risk."

"Then lead the way, if that is what you feel is best. I'm still not certain going alone is wise, though." Evera said, waving her left hand outward.

As Evera closed and locked the door behind her, Lorkai said, "It is still early. I think we can slip out unnoticed."

"Well, it's not like anyone will ask questions," Evera shrugged.

"They will once it is realized we have been gone for a long time and haven't checked in. No one must see us."

Their blue cloaks fanned out as the two friends hurried down the hallways. Very few eyes were alert at this hour. Some guards were posted on duty, but Evera and Lorkai managed to take alternate routes or slink past. The overnight security guard's eyes were glazed over, and he yawned as the wizards tiptoed by. "Wow, I sure feel safe knowing they are keeping watch," Lorkai whispered to Evera, who simply smiled in return. A little over ten minutes later, they had managed to make their way outside. Birds sang merrily, and the sky was quickly brightening. "You know, that was a bit too easy," remarked Lorkai.

"Sadly I will have to agree with you. Especially since we are at war."

"I suppose they figure the worlox are not this far south, and the temples in this region haven't been attacked in years."

"This is just nuts!" Evera exclaimed, shaking her head.

"Having second thoughts already?"

"It's that you've only just arrived, and now we are sneaking out again."

"I can't just leave them."

"I wasn't asking you to," Evera interrupted, "but this all just seems strange… or something. I can't find the right word. Everything feels so off. The Magister is acting strange, and he and the council are obviously hiding way too much, not to mention their lack of concern for our fellow wizards taken captive. Now we are sneaking out of our own temple!"

"Such are the times, Evera. Our leaders refuse to act. It is, therefore, our responsibility to uphold what is moral."

"I hope you're right."

The two friends hastened along the only road from the temple. Muddy puddles still pooled in the gravel from the storm a couple days ago. Tall trees hung over the road, forming a green archway and nearly blocking out the sun. "You know, we should have taken a couple horses. This is going to take forever on foot," Evera moaned.

"That would just alert everyone that much sooner."

"It's just so creepy here. There isn't anyone around for miles. The only things that can be heard are trees groaning and birds singing."

"I kind of like it," said Lorkai.

A flash in the distant sky caught Evera's eye. As she continued walking, she stared, waiting to see if it would happen again. When nothing happened after several seconds, she looked down at her feet, and then out of the corner of her eye, she saw the flash again. Her eyes narrowed, straining to see through the forest growth. Then it happened again. This time she saw it clearly; what looked like a purple lightning bolt flickered in the sky. She craned her neck from left to right trying to get a better view, but the trees continued to block her vision.

"What do you see?" Lorkai asked.

"Didn't you see that?"

"See what?"

"I could have sworn I saw lightning, but it was *purple*."

"You sure?"

"Yes~ah~ I think so. Why? Do you know something about it?"

"We will need to move faster," was Lorkai's only response.

Soon miles lay between them and the temple, and the morning light wore on to the afternoon. The trees gradually thinned. The winds picked up as they moved on, but whether it was due to the lack of cover from the forest or simply the weather, they could not say. One thing was certain: the air was definitely a lot cooler. Evera wrapped her cloak closer and held her arms against her chest. Lorkai, on the other hand, did not seem to notice. He continued with his back straight and his expression stern.

"Are we ever going to take a break?" Evera said after over an hour of silence.

"Huh?" The other turned. "Oh, do you need one?"

"Well we just haven't eaten or rested all day. Not to mention this wind, this horrible wind! It just does not stop."

"So you need to take a break because it's windy?" Lorkai asked, raising an eyebrow.

"No, that's not exactly what I'm saying. It's just that we haven't stopped walking for hours and my feet are really hurting. Maybe we could just set up camp until morning?"

"I guess, but what does that have to do with the wind?" he asked, unable to keep from smiling.

Evera chuckled, elbowing her friend. "You're a jerk."

A fire crackled in the mist of the waning afternoon. Lorkai sat upon a rock. One hand held a piece of dried meat, and the other fingered his facial hair while he chewed. His nostrils flared, and he gazed upon the flames as they greedily licked the timber. Taking another bite, the general finally looked up, a wall of dark clouds was heading their way from the north. "Looks like more rain."

"Those clouds look like they will bring one heck of a storm with them, too. We should probably get going. Hopefully we can find shelter before they let loose," Evera commented as she finished chewing.

"~~Yeah,~~ I suppose you're right, but we will probably be hard-pressed to find any sort of shelter out here. Besides didn't you want to rest for the night?"

"I did until I saw those!" She pointed to the sky.

A streak of bright amethyst flashed in the clouds, accompanied by what sounded like hundreds of war drums beating at once. The sun was quickly shrouded in darkness. All went black, as if night had come early, but there were no stars or moon, just complete blackness. The dense clouds rumbled more and more, and they continually flickered with purple lightning, the only source of illumination.

Evera's ear picked up a shrill hum nearby, and she instinctively slapped at it, all the while watching wide-eyed as the massive storm rolled in. However, the persistent hum simply escalated, until all she could hear was the maddening sound of winged insects. "Evera, we need to move!" Lorkai shouted, jerking his friend, but she didn't move. She merely stood there. Her breathing became shallow as her body started to tremble. All around, thousands of flies swarmed, biting every chance they got as Evera remained motionless. "Evera! Evera! Come on!" Lorkai called out, shaking his friend, but she didn't respond. The air around them vibrated from the sound of wings. The more intense the storm became, the more flies there were. He noticed that blue veiny welts started to form on Evera, but he couldn't see anything of the sort on himself. "Evera! Can you hear me? Evera!" Lorkai's voice cracked, trying to get any sort of response from his friend, but there was nothing.

Lorkai's right hand grasped the hilt of his sword, withdrawing it from its scabbard. His hand tightened around the brown leather handgrip, and then the edges of the blade glinted red and the Goandrian runes etched along the blade glowed like hot embers. Thrusting the weapon into the air, an explosion of red light burst outward, forming a spherical membrane around the two wizards. All flies within collapsed to the ground, and those that touched the light sphere from the outside were instantly struck dead, but still they kept attempting to force their way in. Lorkai's left fingertips glowed as he gently placed them on Evera's forehead. Grimacing, he repeated the process. "Come on, Evera. I can't hold up the shield and protect us at the same time. I need you to snap out of it!" But the woman didn't move. She remained in the same position, staring catatonically while the welts continued to spread across her body. *What do I do? What do I do?* Lorkai thought frantically as he looked around, trying to find something that would give him any sort of answer, yet he found none. Gritting his teeth, Lorkai waved his blade in a figure eight in the air and shouted out a phrase in Goandrian. Suddenly the sphere dissipated and the flies renewed their assault. He knew there were only seconds before he too would succumb to the insects' poison. He placed his left fingertips on his friend's forehead one more time, and Evera's entire body pulsated with light.

Her eyes snapped open, and she gasped. "Lorkai?"

"We got to go, no time to explain!"

Grabbing Evera's arm Lorkai sprinted on as the army of flies perused them. With his right hand, Lorkai held Evera as she struggled to keep pace, and with his left, he grasped his sword. "Evera, I'm gunna need you to keep up with me."

"I'm sorry! I'm trying, I just feel so tired, so…tired," she panted.

Lorkai groaned, hoisting his weapon upward again. The magical sphere reformed as the two collapsed onto the field. A never-ending flow of flies committed suicide as they bombarded the shield again.

"Kai, what are those things! What is going on here? Those aren't normal flies, and this definitely isn't a storm of nature, and you clearly know more than you are letting on. I need answers!"

"I…I didn't want to worry you over something that might not actually be happening!"

"Lorkai, look around. It is happening. I need you to be honest with me."

Lorkai slowly shook his head, his eyes shifting to the ground as he exhaled. "I first saw this several months ago. We were entrenched, digging our heels in and pushing the worlox back, but eventually both sides reached a stalemate. The battlefield was covered with the fallen, as far as the eye could see in any direction. The only thing that any could see were dead wizards and defeated worlox infantry. One day I woke up, it should have been about midday, but there was complete darkness. There were flies everywhere, poisoning our soldiers, and the only light was from an unnatural purple lightning. Then they came, an army larger than I could have fathomed the worlox had ready was unleashed upon us. That was my greatest defeat in all my time as a general. There were two other times I saw this phenomenon as well, and again we were defeated and forced to retreat."

"What are we going to do? The worlox are no longer this far south. Are you saying that we are under attack? Lorkai, we must go back. We must warn the Magister, no matter your differences."

Lorkai's eyes flared, and the corner of his mouth curled. "Go back? There are lives at stake, lives that I was entrusted to protect."

"How many prisoners are there, Lorkai? Is it really worth risking everyone who lives at the temples for the sake of *maybe* rescuing your comrades who were taken captive?"

"Why does everyone keep asking me how many are prisoners? What difference does it make? Besides, what makes you think we can't save everyone," he said, winking with a half-smile forming.

"Wait, what? You're joking. Tell me you are joking. Why were you just arguing with me, then, about turning back?"

"Shhh!" Lorkai abruptly snapped. "They are getting close."

"How can you tell?"

"I hear them faintly, but it's definitely there.

"All I hear is this awful, apparently demonic, storm."

Lorkai tilted his head, and his right eye narrowed. Slowly crouching forward, he motioned his friend to follow. After crawling along for some time, Evera let out a disgusted sigh. "Lorkai, no one is around. I'm getting up."

"Wait," Lorkai hastily grabbed her arm,."The flies, they're gone."

"Isn't that a good thing?"

"Perhaps, but I have never seen that happen before. They just disappeared! What are the worlox up to?"

"Maybe we could get a better look from up there?" Evera pointed to a hill in the northeast that rose higher than the others.

Twenty-minutes later the wizards made it to the summit of the hill. In spite of the surrounding land being covered with grass, this particular hill desired to be unlike its brothers. During the climb, Lorkai and Evera's boots became torn and scuffed, and their fingertips were skinned from jagged rocks. Some rocks were the size one would expect to find, maybe a foot or so in length, and others were large enough to set the foundation for a small family's home. One commonality remained: all were razor sharp, as if Goandria herself forged it out of some sinister plot to mince any who dare climb the hill.

However glad the wizards were when at last they reached the hilltop, the sight before them made the hill seem as welcoming as a warm bed and a feather pillow. Like ants, thousands of black and gray armored soldiers flooded into view. At the head of each battalion lumbered figures standing at least twice as tall as their kinsmen. Evera's eyes widened. "I heard rumors but never thought the berserkers actually existed. Yet here are at least a score of them leading each regiment." She tried to turn her head away, but her eyes refused to obey. The creatures she watched were comprised entirely of blue and white flame, and a crown of mid-sized horns rimmed their heads. One feature was most chilling of all, one that Evera could not stop looking at while at the same time the sight made her stomach turn: the large worlox all had pure black eyes. They were darker than the darkest night, so void of color or light that for a moment, she had an inner debate as to whether or not the creature even had eyes.

"Oh, they exist but rarely come out, and it's even rarer for this many to go into battle," Lorkai said, but Evera responded only with silence.

"Wait," Lorkai blurted, suddenly shaking Evera and pointing downward. "I think we only see half our problem." Evera's eyes shifted to the base of the hill, seeing thousands of worlox infantry storming their way. Others began the ascent up hill. All around, the worlox quickly closed in on the wizards.

Chapter 4

It started as a heavy mist accompanied by tendrils of fog that reached out to cover every area of ground they could find. It was not long before the mist became a sprinkle and the sprinkle became a torrential downpour, as if the heavens themselves had unleashed an ocean of water with rain drops so large and so cold, the wizards wondered if it was hail hitting their armor.

Several helms twisted into the forms of grimacing creatures faced the wizards. Ginger eyes flamed behind the eyeholes, and four horns, measuring about six inches, protruded from beneath the helmets. Their chests heaved in and out as gurgling snarls emanated from behind the masks. In their right hand, each held a completely black broadsword. For all light that touched the black was immediately absorbed within the metal, causing a shadowy aura to form. One worlox was met with a boot smashing into its face, and others were struck down by Lorkai's sword, but another managed to nick the wizard's thigh. Instinctively, Lorkai grasped the wound with his left hand as he continued to fight.

"They just keep coming!" Evera shouted to her friend.

"I know, but I don't know what to do," Lorkai, responded as a blast of green electricity coursed through a half-dozen worlox, reducing them to smoldering ash. Ten more peeked up over the hill top and were also repelled by a green fire blast from Evera.

"They've got the hill completely surrounded!"

"Yes, I see that. Give them everything you got. Don't let up!" Lorkai flashed a wild smile.

The worlox quickly overcame the hill. Now fighting back to back, the wizards' weapons ceaselessly struck against the worlox. Their arm muscles burned, begging for respite. With each stroke, their swords felt heavier. Lorkai gasped for air. His head throbbed, and his vision began to darken. Blood pooled at his feet; his wound was deeper than he previously thought, and black ooze seeped and bubbled out of the gash. *Great, poison*, he thought. Gathering what strength he had, Lorkai pushed back even harder against the demons. His sword glowed red-orange, slicing through the worlox armor, but it did not matter how many fell, for still more came. It felt like an endless tide, and darkness started to cloud Lorkai's consciousness.

Without warning, the fighting ceased. Backing away from the wizards, the worlox infantry all looked at one another and scurried back down the hill. "What's going on?" Evera gasped.

"I, uh, I don't know. Nothing like this has happened to me before," Lorkai stammered just before his knees gave out.

"Lorkai!" Evera rushed over and cradled her friend's head.

"I'll be alright," he said, forcing a smile through the pain.

"No, you won't. Your wound is bad, but I can mend it for now. You will need to get real treatment soon." Evera proceeded to flare her fingers, and a beam of yellow-white light bathed over Lorkai's thigh. "Can you stand now?"

"Ye~~sah~~, I think so. What do you suppose has the worlox so rattled?"

"I think I see the answer," Evera said, nodding westward.

Rising up from the west, another mass of metal-clad figures came forth. Thousands of heavy footsteps clomped. Drums beat from behind the advancing army, setting the pace of the march. At the front of each formation, the standard bore what looked like a four-eyed dragon head with a flaming mane. The banners flailed and whipped as the gale-force winds tore at them, but the pikes which held them would not let them go. The creature depicted on the banners came up from the southern flank. With each step, a blackened footprint the size of a man was left in the grass. Black eyes with streaks of red and orange burned in its skull like hot embers as its eight lids narrowed, surveying the opposing forces. A throaty growl bellowed from the being, revealing yellow and black reptilian-like teeth. The fiery mane which ran from the base of his skull down to the end of his thin rat tail flared brighter. He growled again. this time a spirt of fire shot from his mouth, and the infantry on each side rushed in. Long, black broadswords materialized in their hands as they ran, and bolts of fire unleashed from black bows pelted each side.

"The worlox are now fighting each other?"

"It would seem so, but I have never heard of this. The demons have always seemed so organized, so calculated, so unified." Lorkai shook his head. "There must be something big going on for them to commit their berserkers to the battlefield. Even more bizarre, warlords never fight and never emerge from their sanctums, yet here is one leading the western army himself."

"How do you know that is a warlord if hardly anyone has seen one?" Evera raised an eyebrow.

"When you fight as long as I have, you tend to see things the enemy wishes you didn't. A few years back, I led a secret raid on a sanctum, so secret it was never to be recorded. It was the first time since the worlox invaded that a sanctum had ever fallen."

"A few years ago I would have been there with you."

"You weren't. Trust me," Lorkai said, deepening his voice. "The horrors inside that igloo those creatures called a fortress, and the things they would do to their prisoners…"

The black swords of each side frantically carved at one another. Blue berserkers smashed their way through the infantry of the enemy army, yet the warlord's forces were much larger and hastened to swarm their bigger brethren.

"Look at the warlord. Its frame is far more narrow and nimble than their kind is supposed to be," Evera pointed.

"Yeah," Lorkai shrugged. "What difference does it make?"

"What if he isn't a he at all? I mean we are calling it a warlord, but what if it isn't a lord? What if it's a lady?"

"Impossible. The worlox don't have a sex in the same way people do."

"But there are males and females, though, right?" Evera pressed.

"Well that may be, but only because it reflects the personality of their spirits. Remember they are demons, Evera, not animals. Also, female worlox are very, very rare. They haven't been seen in decades, possibly centuries. Even so, I'm not sure what importance this has."

"That is just it, though. The berserkers, a female warlord (whatever those are called), all of which the worlox have been reluctant to reveal in the past. Major unrest is happening, and they are bringing out the heavy weapons."

Lorkai tilted his head and pursed his lips, "Evera, I think that much is clear. I mean, they are fighting one another, after all."

"What I'm saying is that there has to be so much more going on beneath the surface. This battle is one small part to a greater whole, and if infighting is happening here, where the worlox aren't supposed to be, then where else is it? What if tensions are so high that they can ultimately weaken themselves? Maybe even destroy themselves? This is a blessing, Lorkai. One that we have been waiting for."

"It's an interesting idea. As you implied, though, there are many variables we are unfamiliar with at this point. Hey, at least they don't appear to have any interest in attacking the temple, but the larger issue for the present moment is how we get past the worlox armies."

"Well we can't go through there!"

"No, and I am surprised we have gone undetected this long. If we linger, that luck may run out," Lorkai said.

Below, dozens, possibly hundreds of worlox had fallen on both sides. With each stroke of an ebony blade, another demon dissipated into a black vapor. The infantry snarled and hissed at their rivals, some even resorting to tooth and claw to vanquish their foes. Even in the middle of such destruction, there were some who came out completely unscathed. Those whose bodies blazed with blue and white fire swept aside both friend and foe with each stroke of their weapons. The berserkers each bore war hammers. The handles were six feet long, and on the top was a foot-long slab of iron with a spike on one end rimmed with fire. The nasty weapons tore into the infantry charging at the warlord.

The warlord simply remained motionless, idly watching her foes carving a path to her. Footmen with tower shields bearing her image shuffled around their mistress, forming a wall that encircled her. As soon as the shield-wall was constructed, she lifted her hands, and from her outstretched fingertips, an array of blackness shot out. Two swirling vortexes entangled themselves amongst the rival soldiers, darker than the night itself. No light could penetrate them, and all they touched were consumed by the darkness. Berserker or footman, it did not matter. All fell before the darkness.

"What is she doing?"

"Who cares? This is our chance to get out of here!" Lorkai exclaimed.

As hastily as the sharp stone would allow, the wizards climbed down the eastern side of the hill. This time though, Lorkai's leg burned with every movement. Blood continued to flow from the wound covering his leggings, making the descent feel like an insurmountable challenge. When the climb was over, Lorkai turned his palms upward with his fingers half curled. The pads of his fingertips were scored and bloodied and deep gouges crisscrossed along his palms. Moreover, the cut on his thigh started to ooze with a sticky black liquid again. Grimacing, he knelt down at the base of the hillside and gently waved his right hand above the left. "Ah!" he shrieked, reactively pulling his right hand away. When the throbbing pain subsided some, he attempted the procedure again, even more gingerly. Yet again nothing happened.

"It won't work! Why can't I do a simple healing?"

"Hey, you don't need to get so upset," Evera said kindly. "Calm down and focus,"

Lorkai noticed his friend's hands did not have a blemish on them. "How did you do that so fast?"

Evera raised her eyebrows, and her gaze met Lorkai's. "You need to focus."

"You do not need to keep repeating yourself, Evera! I have been a wizard far longer than you, and I am well aware of what I need to do. Your patronizing advice offers little aid," Lorkai snapped. Once more his right hand hovered over the other with the same result. "Ugh!" he flew into a rage and without warning, a fiery blue explosion erupted around him. Before the blast reached Evera, a dome of energy enclosed around her.

"Lorkai! Whether you want to hear it or not, you need to calm down. You could have killed me!" Stomping over, she spread her fingers over Lorkai's injuries. A yellow-white light bathed over the cuts, causing them to instantly disappear. "There, your hands are better now, but the cut you got from the worlox blade looks like it is getting worse. Can you walk?"

"Yes, I've dealt with worse," Lorkai said shyly.

"Now, would you care to tell me what all that was about?"

"Look around you. The world is falling apart. I was chosen by the wizard council to lead us to victory, but I can't even save my soldiers who were captured. We haven't been gaining any ground against the worlox, and with this act of defiance, I am most likely going to be discharged from the military, perhaps even the wizard order itself. So much is expected of me, and I couldn't even muster up a healing spell."

"You are putting too much pressure on yourself. You cannot do everything. One step at a time, Kai. One step at a time. Let's just focus on getting past these worlox because, in case you hadn't noticed, we still aren't past them."

"I'm sorry, Evera. You didn't deserve the way I treated you. You keep me grounded. It's just sometimes I feel so *limited*. Do you ever wonder why Voshnore never gave us more power to work with?"

Evera's head cocked a bit, and she slowly licked her lips. "I think the answer to that question is obvious. There must always be limits. The greater the power, the greater the limits. Now, I think that is a discussion for another time. Right now we really need to go."

Unseen by the warring demons, the wizards scurried along the eastern edge of the grassy field, just barely out of the worlox's sight. By the time Evera and Lorkai were past, the army that marched out of the east had been utterly decimated. Smoldering black armor lay strewn about the field, and what once was green was now reduced to charcoal and ash. Small flickers of flame licked the ground, and embers glistened, desperate for any source of food, but little remained. The warlord sifted her way through the remains of the fallen. A few of the helms she nudged with her feet, gazing expressionlessly upon the thousands of metal pieces. Without a word, she lifted her left hand and curled it into a fist. Immediately the lightning ceased and the stars shone through to welcome the new night. Then, silently, she marched to the head of her army, the lesser worlox quickly shuffling out of the way and bowing their heads as she passed. Once at the head of the army, the warlord raised her left fist again, and the soldiers marched in unison behind her.

Inching forward, Lorkai, scanned the area and came upon a pile of armor which lay smoldering in the burnt grass with ash strewn about. Crouching down, he dipped his middle finger into the remains of the worlox and rubbed it around with his thumb. Looking northwest, the wizard saw that the army was already almost out of sight. "They apparently are not concerned about our temple at all. A force that size could give us a lot of trouble, if not wipe us out," he said. The wind danced through the grasses, combing through Lorkai's hair as he stood back up. Taking a deep breath, he closed his eyes for a second, allowing the sounds of nature to fill his ears and the cool breeze to invigorate his lungs.

"Isn't that good, though?" Evera's voice broke through.

"I don't know." Lorkai shook his head, staring at the army as it moved over the horizon. "I feel like there is something more, like we should be concerned that the worlox are fighting one another, but I have no good explanation for it."

"No matter what, there is nothing we can do about it right now. We should probably try to get some sleep while the night is still young."

Lorkai smirked. "You never were able to stay up late."

"You need to get some sleep too. If you don't, your leg might just force you to. You don't just have a little scratch, Lorkai. You were poisoned."

"Stop worrying about me." Lorkai waved nonchalantly. "It looks much worse than it really feels, but like always, you are probably right. Here is as good a place as any to sleep for the night as long as another worlox army doesn't pass through." In spite of what came out of his mouth, the reality was that burning tendrils of pain wrapped around his leg and shot throughout the whole left side of his body. He felt lightheaded. He doubted he would ever be able to sleep, but at the same time he half-expected to pass out at any moment. Once Evera was curled up on the ground, buried beneath her cloak, he peeled back the leather around his cut, examining it with a grimace and a sharp intake of breath. "Here goes…" he sighed. His hands trembled as Lorkai suspended them over the wound. Again he took another deep breath. "Come on!" Once more, he lifted his hands and shut his eyes. This time a yellow-white light shone from his palms and shrouded the wound. Several moments passed, but the wound did not look any different. Then, the pain intensified, like liquid fire coursing through his body. "Ah! Evera! Help, help!" he shrieked in terror before slipping out of consciousness.

Goandria: The Schism

Part II

Chapter 1

"Lorkai!" Evera shook him. "Lorkai, wake up!" But the wizard remained unresponsive.

Again she used her healing spell on him, but his eyes did not open. Evera rapidly paced back and forth while combing her fingers through her hair and then knelt back down at her friend's side. "Lorkai, what did you do?" She checked his pulse, then released a small sigh of relief. One more time, Evera spread her hands over Lorkai's body, and a yellow-white light bathed over him, but still the wound looked the same. "Come on, Lorkai. You are the strongest person I know. You have fought more times than any against the worlox, this cannot be the end!" Her eyes reddened. Collapsing onto Lorkai, Evera wept bitterly. "I cannot lose you too. You give me strength and hope in this dark world. Lorkai, what can I do? Tell me how to save you, just please…"

Then Lorkai moaned. Perking up, she stopped sobbing and listened. Her eyes unblinkingly stared into the other's face. She held his hand, praying what she heard was real. "Ev..er..a?" Lorkai moaned, turning his head slightly toward her. "Lorkai!" She blurted out, throwing her arms around him.

"Ow!"

"Ooh, sorry, sorry!"

"Oh, my head…"

"What happened?"

"The last thing I remember was trying a healing spell and suddenly being in the worst possible pain I could ever imagine."

"You mean your own powers did this? How are you feeling now?"

"I feel like I got hit in the head with a hammer, but it's too soon to tell with my leg. I really don't know what happened. When I tried healing myself, it didn't work. Then, suddenly, it looked like it was going to, and then darkness." Lorkai's eyebrows furrowed, looking around frantically. "Wait, it was night. The last thing I remember, it was night. How long was I out?"

"I woke up, thought I heard you screaming, but when I saw you, you were just lying there. I thought I was dreaming, so I rolled over. When I woke up again, I just had a strange feeling. I tried waking you up, but you didn't answer. I guess I didn't even notice the sun rising. I was so worried about you."

"Uh, we've already lost so much time, but I'm so tired. I just need an hour or two, and then I think I can make it to the next settlement."

"You can't be serious. We need to turn back now. The temples are better prepared to heal your wound than we are."

"I'll be fine, Evera."

"You said that before! Clearly you were lying to me. Stop trying to be tough, and be honest with me. If you weren't in so much agony, I'd knock you upside the head."

"I don't doubt that."

After nearly two hours, Lorkai woke up to light rain sprinkling his face. The morning sun was overshadowed by a quilt of gray and white. Lorkai silently limped over to his weapons and slung his now-muddy cloak around him.

"How are you doing? And answer honestly this time," Evera said.

"Better than expected. How long was I asleep?"

"Longer than you had hoped, but I figured you needed the rest. Now please, answer the question without brushing it aside. It's important because if you are this determined to keep going, I need to know you are actually going to make it there," Evera said.

Lorkai looked at his feet and exhaled. "My head is fine. It feels a little foggy though, and my leg is still throbbing. I think I can manage for now, though. It doesn't really matter anyway because we are committed now."

"~~Yeah,~~ I guess we are, but with our now-ruined boots and your injuries this journey just became even more insane."

A fire danced in the corner, reflecting off a woman's wrinkled face as she sat perched in an armchair with a needle in hand. Ten paces away in the cozy home, another woman stood over a stove, stirring ingredients in a pot vigorously with one hand while tossing in more chopped vegetables with the other. When everything was added, the woman spooned some out and let it dribble out of the utensil. "It is so hard to get the right consistency," she complained, but the other woman merely grunted in response, engrossed in her needlework. Hastening to the other end of the kitchen, the floor creaking beneath her feet, the cook grabbed a white powder and tossed it into the pot. "There. That should help." She fiercely stirred the contents again. A few moments passed. "That should do it. We are gunna have a fine stew today." She beamed, again noticing nothing more than a few grunts from the other woman. This time the cook turned to her, hands on hips and eyes wide and reddening. She blurted out, "May, when are you going to put that down? You have been working on that so long now, you probably don't even know what it's supposed to be anymore."

The seamstress did not even glance up; she kept going with her work.

"May, you listening? I slave over the stove, and I clean our home, and all you do is sit there, only saying something if you need something.

"So? I don't ask you to, and it isn't like you have anything better to do. Neither of us do now," May said.

"Ever since he died, you have been talking such nonsense! Isn't it time you start living again?"

Before the other could answer, a knock pounded against the door. "Hello?" A female voice called on the other side.

"Who could that be?" May perked up.

"Dunno. It ain't like the village to come knocking on our door. Must be something serious." The cook shuffled to the door. The chocolate-brown door screeched loudly as it pivoted open on iron hinges. On the front stoop was a young woman supporting a young man who was slumped down with closed eyes and wheezy, labored breathing.

"Goodness what have we here?" the old lady gasped.

"We are wizards traveling northward. My friend is badly hurt and in need of any medicine you might be able to spare."

"Wizards in these parts? Your kind hasn't been this way since I was young."

"Yvonne, don't pester them with such useless nonsense!" May snapped from the cottage.

"Oh, you're right, you're right! Come in. Lay your friend down on the couch over there. My sister and I will have a look at him."

"How did you find us out here? Travelers avoid this village, most don't even know we are still around, and if you are wizards, why isn't he healed already?" May asked.

"I'm a scholar at the nearby temples. There aren't any settlements that are secret to me. As for your second question, he was cut by a worlox weapon that was apparently poisoned with something we have never encountered before. Our magic won't work to heal him. When he tried to mend his own wound, it backfired and nearly killed him."

"Still, how did you know to come here? Either you know more than what's good for you or you are incredibly lucky. When the worlox were more interested in managing every person's lives, one of the town's folk was poisoned by this very same thing. Black goo running out of sores that formed, barely lucid. However, I managed to come across an herb that counteracted the stuff. Mostly though, the demons would put it in their target's food supply. This is the first I have heard of it being used on weapons. You say you have never seen this before, and you are wizards?"

"I haven't at least. I'm not sure if he has. It's been a while since I fought actively in the war," Evera said.

"May! Now who is jibber-jabbering?"

"An herb, you said, will heal him, and you said you have dealt with this before? That seems awfully convenient. We knew to come to this village because we figured there was more hope here than staying in the wild while he was in this condition," Evera said.

"I guess it is more of a weed than an herb that grows around here occasionally. I'm going to have to take a look and see if we still have some." May hobbled over to the pantry.

"May! Stop, I don't think that is going to help him. No, no this is something else. It looks similar, but it isn't the same thing that we have had before," Yvonne called back.

"What? Now what do we do?"

"All we can do is make him comfortable right now. We will try to figure out something, but there is not much we can do. The good news is that if anyone can help him, we are probably the only ones for a hundred miles, except for maybe your wizards at the temples."

"Yvonne, he is burning up!"

"Then go get some water," Yvonne snapped. "So what are your names?"

"My name is Evera, and this is Lorkai."

"You probably already figured it out by now, but I'm Yvonne, and my sister's name is May."

Evera watched Yvonne squeeze a rag filled with cold water over Lorkai's face. The wizard stirred some, which his friend took as a good sign. A few indecipherable moans and groans came out of Lorkai's mouth, and then he settled back down. It looked as if he was fast asleep, perhaps even comfortable. *I wonder what he's thinking? Maybe nothing at all.*

What Evera didn't know was that Lorkai could hear everything going on around him, but what he saw was not the small house, his friend, or the old women. Alone in a shallow hole, Lorkai sat with his knees pressed against his chest. One arm wrapped around his legs, and the other gripped his sword hilt so tightly his knuckles turned white. Violet droplets softly splashed against his armor, lightning disrupted the cloudless sky, and a sense of danger lurked, yet he did not know why. Growls echoed in the distance. Flattening out on the ground, Lorkai peeked out of his hole. He found himself in the midst of a horde of worlox. Time slowed as the enemy's weapons bore down on him. Tendrils of a blue and white smoky mist felt their way along the ground, encompassing all.

Lorkai looked around quickly, trying to make sense of the situation, but his mind felt hazy, and nothing was clear to him. A voice whispered in his ear, "I told you, didn't I? I told you that I am your future. I am the power you will one day have. Deny me all you like. I know you. I am you. We don't want to be helpless anymore. We don't want to be pawns of the wizards." The voice was cold and raspy, as if an icy blanket had been wrapped around him.

"You are not me. You are something dark, something else. I want nothing to do with you and your promises!" Lorkai screamed.

"But I am you! I am the part of you that wonders if being a wizard is even the right path to victory in this war. I am the part of you that grows weary of the limitations on our power. I have seen your future, and I will guide you through it. I will bring victory in this war, and I will help you conquer Goandria! I am your true self, your full potential. The person Evera thinks she knows has been dying slowly ever since you first fought on front lines without her."

"This isn't right. Last I remember, I was at the door of a small house with my arm around Evera's shoulder. I'm dreaming!" Lorkai gasped, his eyes wide, and the worlox army was snuffed out. He found that he sat in total darkness. There was no floor, no walls, no sky, nothing but blackness and a blue and white lupine creature.

"That makes little difference, for what I say is true," the wolf taunted.

"It makes all the difference. You aren't real, just in my mind."

"Haven't you been listening? I *am* you! You can try to suppress me, ignore me, and pretend I do not exist, but you know I am the real you."

"Shut up! You are nothing but my imagination, probably some suppressed fear or maybe a manifestation of all the horrors I have seen."

"That is what you keep telling yourself. You do not want to admit who you really are. You are not quite ready to do what it takes to obtain ultimate power. I am the part of your personality that will lead you to victory. One day, you will rule all of Goandria. You will be immortal, an invincible god amongst mortals. The sooner you stop denying me, the sooner that power will become yours. You will embrace a whole new power that will bring forth a new era."

If asked, Lorkai would say that the words he heard were revolting and that he was not tempted at all. However, deep down he knew it was all lies he was telling himself. Lorkai's heart leapt at the thought of having so much power at his disposal, to finally have his way. No longer would he have to answer to a council or a magister. He would be his own. He would be lord and master. No longer restrained by the confines of being a wizard, he would be evolved beyond a wizard. The wolf was gone. A tall, black-armored warrior marched toward him. "I am your future," a deep voice thundered behind the helm.

With a gasp, Lorkai's eyes opened.

"Lorkai!" Evera rushed over.

"Uhh, I feel terrible," Lorkai groaned.

"I can imagine. I was beginning to think you wouldn't wake."

"How long this time?"

Evera's face scrunched just for a second. "What?"

"How long was I out this time?"

The woman frowned. "You shouldn't make light of it, Lorkai."

"Why not? I've been in and out of consciousness so much and losing time over such a ridiculous wound."

"You were poisoned. That is far from ridiculous, but anyway, you were out about two days. You had a terrible fever. Sometimes you would shake or call out, but none of us could understand you."

Lorkai gazed off at the window. His chest rose and fell slowly as he lay there motionless, unblinking. His leg burned, but it was far less sore than earlier. Lorkai's mind replayed the vision he just had, the promises of power, the underlying feeling of helplessness. The wolf specter was eerie, but the wizard knew deep down that it spoke the truth. A slight chill came over him, and he remained quiet, no longer paying Evera any mind or even knowing if she was still talking to him. He still doubted what he saw was anything more than his own mind projecting its desires, but he wondered what it all meant. Was he really that dark inside? Was this how he felt all along? Was he doing the right thing? Doubt gnawed its way into his mind, continually pressing more and more upon his thoughts. *What if there is another way to power outside of the wizards? But Voshnore had forbidden the use of the powers he bestowed outside of his dogma. I've never heard of it, but is there, maybe, a way to transcend being a wizard? What if the wolf was right, and this is the only way to defeat the worlox?* As he lay there, immersed in his own thoughts, fatigue began to set in once more. "Tired again. I'm always tired," he said to himself as he yawned.

"How are you doing, honey?" an old woman's voice cut through his thoughts.

"All I want to do is sleep, but I've already done so much of that."

"Shut your eyes then. It will take you a long time to heal from what you are going through," May said, but Lorkai was asleep before she finished her sentence.

"How long before he is better?" Evera asked, her eyebrows narrowed and her face tight while she stared at Lorkai.

"Hard to say. We are just lucky we found something that works," Yvonne responded.

"He isn't completely out of danger yet," May added.

"What exactly did you do?"

The two old women glanced at each other. "You've had a hard day worrying about your friend. Why don't you go to bed? We have to make a quick trip to the market, but we won't be gone long. We will wake you if anything happens."

Evera smiled, "Thank you so much for everything you have done."

Flashing smiles of their own, the sisters hurriedly shut the door behind them. Once they were several yards from the house, Yvonne quickly checked over her shoulder and said, "Do you think it worked?"

"You are always the worrier."

"I think I have good reason to! If they knew what we used and the side-effects it could have, they would march us into their temple. Such means of *handling* things are banned by the wizards," Yvonne whined.

"What were we to do, just let him die?"

"If it comes to our freedom, then yes. Or there are other ways to take care of them if the need arises," Yvonne said softly.

Chapter 2

Large flakes slowly sailed down onto the ice encrusted stonework. Along the battlements, in the courtyard, and down the towers ice ran. It was on the ground, the armor of the sentries, and even the hills. It was as ubiquitous as trees in a forest. Such was the weather in the north, an endless and merciless testament to the power of winter. Some say things were not always this way. Whispers spread throughout the villages that in times before the worlox, the north was a place of farming and cities and was no stranger to warmth. Others passed it off as nothing more than legends passed down by lazy people with nothing better to do than spin fairy tales of the past.

The mysteries of the northern region were only compounded by the fact that only worlox dared to venture that way. It was the first area to be completely purged of people during a time when humans and englifs fought alongside the wizard order. The armies that opposed the worlox had been vanquished, but the southern settlements were allowed to continue so long as no one dared to raise arms against the worlox overlords again.

It was in the north that the icy fortress stood out in the midst of the snowy landscape. There were five towers in all, one in the center surrounded by the remaining four. The citadel spiraled skyward, shaped like an asymmetrical cone of ice, snow, and graystone. The smaller towers mirrored this design, but they were narrower, giving the impression of needles rising up from the snow. A hexagonal wall of dark-gray, nearly black, stone enclosed the towers, completing the fortress. Beneath the central tower, far below even the deepest dungeons, seven worlox took their seats in a ring of high-backed chairs.

One worlox narrowed all four of his eyes and shifted his jaw, waiting for the right time. The eyes and fiery manes of the gathered worlox were all that was visible. Damp soil clung to the worlox's feet, a dampness that permeated the darkness in which they all gathered. No fires burned. Not even a single candle was found in the entire fortress, just frigid darkness everywhere. The air was so heavy that it felt like breathing underwater for any who wasn't one of the demons. When the straggling sands in the hourglass finally filtered to the bottom, the demon stood up, "You know why we have gathered today. There are more *situations* pressing upon our rule. The wizards are pressing onward, and the belligerent animals have become more of a nuisance. Adding to this, we have one of our own who is attempting to claim our empire for herself. This insurrection has not been taken seriously and has been allowed to gain traction. Now one of our armies has been decimated by this threat," a warlord said.

A long snarl came from another sitting adjacent to the one who just spoke. "It is of no consequence. None are able to contend with us. We are the never-ending darkness."

"He has valid concerns. This meeting should have happened sooner. The rogue one has enough power to be a threat. What if she attempts to send us back *there?*" another said with a shiver.

"She wouldn't dare! We would carve her up before she would ever get the chance," a worlox sitting on the far side of the room growled.

"It is time that we hit all of our enemies hard. We should send out the berserkers. A whole army of them could eliminate the wizards," added another warlord.

"Vox is right," the one who opened the meeting began. "The berserkers are hungry for action, and if we unleash them upon the wizards, they will stand no chance."

Amongst those present in the darkness were four warlords, but three were completely hidden save for their voices. This particular kind of worlox was the embodiment of shadow and night, for even though they took on solid forms, all light was extinguished in their presence. Though the blackness hid them, they were shaped like men, but slightly taller. It was one of these that spoke next, with a deeper voice than the others. "There are other means we can use to demoralize our foes. Let us not forget the secret army we have."

"They have not been forgotten, but caution must be used if we are to employ them. Also, we are not certain if they are completely loyal to us yet, Rellin."

"What of their general? The insect has become rather bothersome. He is nearly worshipped by his own kind due to his victories against us. If he knows of that army, it could provoke him in unforeseen ways," said Vox.

"Do you propose we dare fear one human wizard?" A shadowy worlox countered.

"No, remember, I suggested we crush the wizards, but we must attempt to look at all possible outcomes, and it would be counterproductive to empower the wizards instead of demoralize them."

"Are we to be frightened of a few dissidents and a rebellious faction of our own kind? We are the gods of this realm! Remember when we first came and quickly crushed the pathetic attempts to stop us? The worlox fear nothing because the worlox *are* fear. Even having this discussion proves that we are too complacent, too comfortable. It is time we remind Goandria what we are. The vermin who populate this land have been reduced to a manageable size, except for the wizards. They should be our primary focus. This insurgent is nothing and will ultimately fall into line on her own or be destroyed in the crossfire," a warlord said, rising to his feet as he addressed the others.

"Charos, your passion is noted, but what you said doesn't offer any real solutions. Diminishing the situation before us is a recipe for our downfall. Goandria, and our place in it, has evolved since our arrival, and we must take that into account. What worked for us in the past may not again. I suggest subtlety combined with force. We have one advantage on our side: even after centuries of us fighting with the wizards, our enemies still understand very little about us. If we take on human forms, infiltrate the wizard ranks across Goandria, spy on them, and sow chaos through exploitation and selfishness, it will weaken them," Vox added.

Rellin hissed as Vox finished, "Charos is right, Vox. If we speak of them as if they can do us harm, then we legitimize that reality. It is unfortunate that when we came here, we were not aware that Voshnore empowered some of his mutants to help protect the world."

A hush fell upon the worlox. All eyes were upon Rellin. "How dare you mention that name here? He who defiles all we fight for and have fought for in the distant past. He who brings about vermin and dares to humiliate us further by granting them a bit of power. You have been warned, Rellin, never speak that name here again, for the purity of our darkness must remain, and we have all sworn to uphold that," said a warlord who was seated next to him. Then turning to the others, he said, "We will not all agree on a solution, but we must put to a vote what we are to do about the wizards and the rebellious one."

"Shall we proceed with might? To render our foes helpless by escalating the war?" Rellin asked. Three nodded.

"And who feels we need to use other tools along with war, such as infiltrating our enemy's ranks?" Vox asked. Five nodded this time.

"Won't the rebellious one know if we infiltrate her army?" Rellin asked.

"She will if she maintains her current power, but we all know that isn't possible if we cut her off from the fissures that connect our world to this one," Charos said.

"That would be difficult, considering she was once a part of the governing *Citheara*," another shadowy worlox spoke up.

"Another concern that has yet to be brought up: she was one of us, a ruler of the mighty worlox, and she wanted more. How can we trust that our generals, or even us as members of the Citheara, will not join her or split off, forming another faction, causing further infighting?" said Vox.

"Her blasphemies are the result of not having a singular vision for the worlox. If we maintain the same goals, such rebellions will not happen," Rellin sneered.

Vox glowered at Rellin, "Sarcasm has no place here. Remember who you are addressing."

"I was only trying…" Rellin began, but Charos cut him off.

"We know what you were doing. Remember what happened to the last one who held a position here and could not keep his mouth shut when appropriate." Then the warlord addressed the rest of the group. "Any more traitorous actions from our own will be dealt with as with any other enemy, and that is all that needs to be said. No foe has been able to stand against and win in the long run."

"As far as I'm concerned, the matter is closed. If there are any further concerns, now is the time to bring them up," Vox said. A few, particularly Rellin, shifted in their seats, but no one said anything.

"Good, then what was discussed here today will be implemented immediately," Charos added.

All members of the Citheara took their leave, save for Rellin and another shadow worlox named Anif. "Something on your mind, Anif?" Rellin's voice hissed.

"You're thinking it too, aren't you?" Anif sneered.

"What?"

"Oh don't play dumb with me. We are brothers after all, and you have never been a difficult one to read, especially for me." Anif chuckled.

"You use the family card when you were never much of family to begin with, cute. That doesn't answer what you are getting at."

"They are fools, Rellin, utter and complete idiots that have no business ruling the worlox people. The worlox have always been about strength and domination. What do you suppose this new approach that Vox has suggested will send? I will tell you: it will send the message to our enemies that we are weak! Now, was I right? That is what you are thinking, isn't it?"

"Of course it is, but what do you plan to do about it? Complaining clearly is not going to help us. We need a strategy," Rellin said.

"We must join with the one who rebelled. It is the only logical thing to do. If we combine our armies with hers, we could eliminate the Citheara. Once that happens, we could kill the rebel leader, and then we would be the lords of the worlox!" Anif declared.

"Bold words spoken from someone who has never taken action before in his life. How do I know this isn't all a set-up? You could be testing me, seeing if I am truly loyal to the Citheara. Even if I agree with you, why would I ever want to partner with you? You are a slimy snake that is only out for himself. The first chance you get, you would stab me in the back," Rellin retorted.

"That is unfair, brother. We may not have agreed on everything, but on this, we do. I can tell you are fed up with the others. You have wondered what it would be like to join her, haven't you? I'll tell you what. If you are interested in my offer, meet me in the courtyard in two hours. If not, then your hands will be clean from any accusations of being a traitor." Anif took his leave.

Unbeknownst to Anif and Rellin, tucked away in a small nook where wondering eyes rarely venture, Vox lay in wait. All four of his dark eyes narrowed as he listened to the conversation between the brothers. Once Anif departed, Vox crept from his hiding spot, blending into the shadows.

Chapter 3

Wind howled against the petite house, and more dark clouds threatened to swallow the morning sunlight and shroud Goandria in gray and rain. Evergreens flailed with each gust, and small rodents scurried to find shelter. All knew that the weather was very likely to turn unpleasant. Evera sat alone at Lorkai's side. Yvonne and May were out once again while Lorkai rested.

"I hate all this lying around," Lorkai grumbled. "I feel so useless. It has been two days since we came here, and all I am capable of is sleep and more sleep."

Evera smiled wearily. "You need it though." She then turned her head to check the window. "Ever notice the old ladies are gone a lot lately? We are total strangers, yet they leave us here for hours at a time."

Lorkai managed a small shrug. "It's a small village, and they are probably more trusting here than the other places we've been."

"And where are they always off to? They don't seem to be the type that have many friends. The whole thing is just very odd," Evera continued, not paying Lorkai's comments any heed.

"Maybe I'm just too tired, but I do not think it's all that weird. They did take us in, and they helped me when they didn't have to. I think that is all that matters," Lorkai said.

"You're probably right. I am looking forward to when we can move on, though."

"How do you think I feel?" Lorkai smirked. "Hey, why don't you get out and explore the village? There is no need for both of us to be stuck inside here."

"I'm fine. I just want you to get better. I haven't really had the chance to get bored yet."

Lorkai took his friend's hand. "Seriously, I want you to have some fun. I will be fine here. I will probably take yet another nap. Besides, we both need new boots, *badly*."

"Are you sure? I'm fine staying here with you."

"Yes. Now go, if for nothing else than to buy us some new boots. We both know that traveling in what we have isn't possible anyway."

"I will try not to be gone too long. Besides, it looks like the weather won't let me spend much time at the market."

A dozen buildings huddled around in a U-shape, with the leather smith at the bottom of the U. In front of the leather smith, two boys and a girl frolicked along, giggling as they swung their wooden swords at one another. Occasionally one of them would manage a particularly swift jab, causing an outburst from another, but they soon resumed their play as if nothing had happened. Mostly women were out at this time of day, several at a time talking with store owners, and all present were bundled in furs and leather. Some had fuzzy hats, and others had long, thick hoods that draped over their faces. A few male voices were heard complaining to store owners about the prices, while other men seemed content spending their time talking in the armory.

It was nearly a twenty-minute walk from Yvonne and May's house to the market, and with every minute that passed, the wind continued to whip through Evera's cloak harder and harder. Wrapping her arms tightly across her chest, she shivered violently. Each exhale appeared as a puff of smoke expelled from her lungs. The unmistakable aroma of leather filled the air, leading Evera to the leather smith's wooden shop. Boards creaked beneath her frayed boots. The wooden floor was made of irregularly shaped pieces, and the various colors seemed to indicate the carpenter simply used whatever was available. The boards were graying and dark, and some had holes in them where bugs had eaten through. In the back left corner sat an iron wood-fueled stove, cylindrical in shape and about two-feet in diameter. All sorts of leather and fur clothing was displayed on the back wall and on one lonely stand in the middle of the store. Jerkins, coats, textile armor, shoes, and boots took up as much space in the tiny building as the owner could fill neatly.

Even the burning hot stove in the corner was no match for the harsh wind that continued to flail the merchant's goods, occasionally knocking an item off the shelf. Evera stood closer to the stove, spreading her hands over the fire, trying to get whatever relief she could from the unrelenting gusts of cold air.

"Is there something I could help you find? Maybe a new coat? It looks like that cloak is not warm enough for these parts," a deep, but kind, voice said from behind the counter.

The leather smith was very tall, standing over six-and-a-half feet tall, and he had a brown beard with streaks of red that reached his belly. A brown, hooded, fur coat concealed the rest of him, hanging all the way down to his feet.

"Yes, I am looking for some boots to buy for myself and my friend."

The leather smith's right eye narrowed slightly as his bushy eyebrows came together in the center. "You are a wizard! We don't get many of your folk here in Grivear."

"So I've been told."

"Well, as you can see, I have a few different types of boots. I can assure you that whatever you get here will be far warmer than what the wizard order issues, not to mention they will last quite a bit longer."

"I'm not looking for anything too fancy, and neither is my friend. We just want something that will protect us," Evera said.

"Then these shall do fine," he said, pulling down a pair of simple black boots that came up to her mid-calf.

After trying them on and walking back and forth a few steps, Evera said, "They fit very well. I do not think any resizing will be needed."

"I wish that could be the case for your friend. For obvious reasons, if you buy a pair for him, I cannot guarantee they will fit," he said.

Evera proceeded to unbutton a pack that was slung over her shoulder. "It's lucky I brought his old pair then." She handed the tattered boots to him.

"I'm pretty sure he would want something similar. Do you think you can manage that?"

The leather smith ran his large, sausage-like fingers over the boots. "Yes, I think so. Come back tomorrow, and they should be ready."

"Thank you." Evera smiled and gave him a couple pieces of silver.

Outside, more people braved the weather and clustered into the tiny market. Light droplets began to fall from the now-dark sky. Then in the corner, her eye caught a glimpse of something familiar. A couple of white-haired ladies were bickering in front of the produce stand. One was slightly taller than the other, both were somewhat hunched over, and the lady on the right seemed to want to argue with everything the other said.

"Yvonne, May?" Evera called out, walking quickly toward the women.

The sisters immediately dropped what they were doing, each one putting on an obviously fake smile as their guest approached them. Instinctively, Evera pursed her lips, then chewed on the lower one. She decided not to pay it any mind. There could be a number of reasons why May and Yvonne seemed so secretive, and by the time Evera reached them, she had put her suspicions out of her mind entirely.

"How is Lorkai?" May asked.

"He is recovering fast but is still worn out much of the time. I have never seen anyone recover this quickly after becoming so ill. You two have some real talent." Evera smiled, but once again, she noticed the old ladies glancing at each other, their expressions hard. The wizard felt as if something was amiss that she could not quite place, but she rationalized again that she was probably just reading into things where there was nothing to be found.

"As long as he will be healthy again soon. I am glad our methods were able to help. Like I said when we met you, you were lucky to have stumbled upon us. Your friend would undoubtedly be dead by now if you hadn't," May said.

"What are these methods that you use? Maybe the wizards could learn something? I mean, neither Lorkai's nor my own magic could heal the poison in his wound."

"What difference does it make? As long as he is on the mend, you should be grateful, and since he is feeling better, I trust that you two will soon be on your way. Our home is small and we have few provisions. Once Lorkai is on his feet, you need to leave," Yvonne snapped.

Taken aback, Evera silently turned and walked off. *It would probably be better to find an inn nearby than continue to stay with a couple of erratic old women. They are covering something up, and I don't trust them. I sure hope Lorkai is well enough to leave either today or tomorrow,* Evera thought.

When she got back to the house, Lorkai was still sleeping, and he continued to sleep through the entire night and well into the morning. May and Yvonne got home sometime in the middle of the night. When Evera got up, May greeted her warmly and offered a small bit of vegetable soup. Evera accepted, her eyes resting on the women as she spooned the soup into her mouth. *I wonder if they know I'm suspicious of them.* Her mind reeled at the possibilities. She considered they were rogue wizards or maybe witches, but nothing seemed to add up. They seemed kind, but at the same time, there was something unsettling about them. It did not take long before the aged women went back to the market for several hours again. Shortly after the creaky door closed, Lorkai's eyes opened.

"Nice to see you finally awake." Evera smiled.

"It's nice to *be* awake. Wow, the sun is high already!" Lorkai groaned, looking outside.

"You needed to sleep. Are you feeling better?"

"Much!" Lorkai slowly swung his feet off the couch and stood up. Evera rushed over to support him as he took his first wobbly steps.

"It's amazing. The pain in my leg is totally gone. I just feel a little weak."

"Do you think you are ready to leave? Yvonne made it clear yesterday that they want us gone as soon as you are ready. If you aren't able to travel yet, we can stay at an inn or something."

"No, no, that won't be necessary. I have laid around far too long as it is. The poor women don't seem to have much, and we have been taking what little they have."

"And there is something going on here. How did they heal you so fast? We couldn't even heal you with our powers, and when I asked them about it, Yvonne just snapped at me. There is more going on than we realize, and I'm concerned about what that might be and, more importantly, the consequences it could have on you."

"Oh, Evera, always the eternal worrier."

"Why can't you just trust me? How would you have any better of a read on them? You were asleep for most of our stay here."

Lorkai flashed a half smirk at his friend. "Indeed I was. What is certain is you have typically had a knack for this sort of thing in the past, and I have looked pretty foolish when I dismissed you. So if you think they are up to something, what do you suggest?"

"What I suggest is that we take a look around and see what we can find."

"Are you sure that is a good idea? What if they come back?"

Evera shrugged. "They are usually gone to the market all day."

"I think this is a bad idea. They did help us when they didn't have to, after all. Digging through their things just doesn't feel right," Lorkai said, but Evera was already at work, rummaging through the cupboards and shelves. Each item she came across, Evera removed from its place, running her fingers over the jars, and checking all sides before putting it back.

"I'm not finding anything other than normal things like food," Lorkai uttered impatiently. "We should probably just get going. Even if the old women are up to no good, I'm starting to think it doesn't matter. I feel better, and they helped us, and that's all that matters."

"Nothing, there is nothing here!"

"Exactly. That's what I just said. Now can we please go?"

Evera sighed. "You are probably right. I'm just being paranoid. They are just a couple of eccentric old ladies and nothing more."

"I don't know, Evera. They might be hiding cat heads in a jar somewhere! Did you check over there? Go on, take a look. You have to check everywhere before we go."

"Oh, be quiet, but since you mentioned it, I think I will take a look."

"Come on, Evera. I was joking!"

"It won't take long. Just give me a minute," she said, pulling out a small wooden crate. Around thirty vials clanked inside the makeshift box every time Evera maneuvered it. She removed the half-broken lid to find the vials contained a black substance. "Lorkai, come take a look at this. What do you think it is?"

"I don't know. Ash or maybe an herb I haven't heard of before?"

Evera took one of the vials and pulled out the cork stopper. "I have a very bad feeling."

"Maybe it is because you are going through someone else's things?"

"No, I mean from this box. There is something not right about it." She dipped the tip of her little finger and immediately dropped the vial. Her body began to convulse, and she collapsed on the floor.

"Evera!" Lorkai called out, rushing to her side.

The spasms only lasted a few seconds. Then Evera stood back up with Lorkai's help. "What just happened? Are you ~~okay~~alright?"

"I think so. Luckily I didn't get much on me. Lorkai, that is worlox ash."

Chapter 4

"Worlox ash? How can that be? Are you sure? What could they possibly be doing with that stuff?" Lorkai gasped.

"I think we know how you were healed so quickly."

"Wait, that is quite the assumption. Nothing good comes from the worlox."

"You know our order bans the use of this, and for good reason, but that doesn't mean it can't be used for good, like healing strangers. The implications of this are pretty scary, Lorkai. We don't know how this will affect you long term."

"But I feel fine, Evera."

"For now, but this stuff is probably very volatile, considering where it comes from."

"I can't believe this." Lorkai shook his head, looking wide-eyed at the vials.

"All I am saying is that we don't know what the long-term result is going to be."

"There have been whispers that people were using this stuff, but I never really believed it. How could someone be so stupid as to use something from the worlox? Have those old women forgotten that we have been fighting a war against those demons or that they persecuted and killed so many people? Evera, we need to find them and get to the bottom of this!"

"Lorkai, calm down. Confronting them while you are angry will only make things worse."

"Worse? I was treated with worlox ashes! How did they even come by this stuff?"

"They spend a lot of time at the market. We should probably look for answers there. Are you sure you are feeling alright?" Evera said.

"Yes, actually, I feel great. Even better than before our fight with the worlox. I have more energy and feel more alert. I'm so angry that something from the worlox was used to treat me, but at the same time, I cannot help but wonder if this wasn't such a bad thing either. I guess I just don't know how to feel about this whole situation."

"I don't either, but at the very least, I would like to know how this stuff is getting into the public and what the ramifications are," Evera said.

Just then, the door groaned open and the ladies stepped through. Yvonne's eyes immediately went to the crate on the floor and the two wizards. "What is going on here?" she screamed.

"Get out! Get out now!" May yelled. "How dare you, when we took you in and did everything we could to save your life?"

"And how could you keep this a secret from us? Don't you know it is illegal to possess worlox ashes for any reason?" Evera countered. "Where did you get all this?"

"I told you to get out!" May screamed so loud her voice cracked.

"We are not leaving until we get some answers. How did you get this stuff, and how will it affect Lorkai?"

"So it has come to this. See, I told you, May. We will have to do whatever is necessary." Abruptly, Yvonne's skin and eyes turned deep black. She appeared to grow larger, as she was no longer hunched over, but fully erect with her arms outstretched before her. "This is your final warning. Leave, wizards, and forget about us and what you found."

May shifted her focus from the wizards to her sister and back again. Her feet slowly propelled her backward. The elderly lady's breathing became more labored, and her eyes widened with each passing moment. Across the room, the wizards had unsheathed their swords, holding them at the ready. Both Yvonne and the wizards glared at one another, waiting for someone to make the first move.

"What are you doing, Yvonne? We don't have to fight. All we want is some answers. This is serious. You are using worlox ashes to imitate the powers of the wizards! Don't you realize they are demons?" Evera pleaded.

"I don't have to give you answers, and I don't have to explain myself! It is the wizards who need to be held accountable. Your kind was tasked with protecting Goandria, and you have failed, yet you continue to fight a losing battle against an unbeatable enemy. While the wizards spread themselves thin and pour all their resources into war, the people are starving. We have no food, no medicine, and we are left to fend for ourselves. Where are the mighty wizards when the crops fail to yield anything, and we are left starving? Sitting in your towers, eating and drinking merrily while the people suffer! We turn to anything we can to give us hope, even if it comes from the worlox. The usage of their remains has done more for this village than any wizard has," Yvonne snarled.

"Fine. Maybe you are right, but turning to this is not the answer!" Evera called out.

"What do you know?" Yvonne cried, as she placed her hands together before her, a ball of black energy forming in her palms. Lorkai shuffled forward, his sword held before him, daring the old woman to attack.

"Yvonne, this is unnecessary. Look at what you are doing. Look at what you have become. Can't you see…" Before Evera could finish, a beam of black energy swirled toward Lorkai. He ducked out of the way just as the magical beam grazed his hair. Without thinking, Lorkai rolled behind Yvonne. For a short instant all was silent and still. He was aware of each heartbeat and every breath as his sword found its mark. The sound of steel against flesh and bone echoed as the blade passed through Yvonne's heart.

"No! What have you done?" May screeched.

"Yvonne, brought this upon herself, May," Lorkai tried to reason, but the wild look on May's face told him that nothing he could say would matter.

"She was right. We never should have brought you in! You wizards are all monsters. Just leave! Leave now and never return to our village."

No more words were exchanged as the wizards stepped out of the small house. Evera glanced behind her. May's body was heaving uncontrollably in the window as she sobbed over her sister's body.

"What a mess." Evera wiped hair out of her face.

"I had no choice. She was going to kill us," Lorkai said.

"I know. I wish it didn't have to come to this," Evera sighed.

"Is it even worth trying to figure out where they got the worlox ash from? I have a feeling the problem is much bigger than we realize."

"I really don't know. Honestly, after what just happened, I'm inclined to say it isn't worth it, but I can't walk away knowing that we could have stopped this from ruining more lives."

"Then what do you suggest, Evera? If we find the one who sells the worlox remains and even manage to find out where he got it from, it won't help us. Remember, we have a mission to save our own who are being held by the worlox. We have already wasted enough time, and now we are so delayed I don't even know if there is any hope to find them alive, or at all for that matter."

Evera exhaled deeply. Her eyes met Lorkai's, but just before she spoke she looked to the sky. A flock of birds flew over the cloud-glazed sun. "You're right. We need to keep moving." She did not take her eyes off the animals until long after they were beyond the horizon.

"I don't feel right about this," Evera said solemnly. "It seems like every decision we make is wrong lately."

"What are you talking about, Evera?"

"We snuck out of the temple, disobeyed the Magister's command to not rescue the prisoners, and left that poor old woman to bury her sister you killed."

"Hey, I told you I had no choice!" Lorkai interrupted defensively.

"I know, I know, Lorkai, but this feels so wrong. I wish we could have helped May. After all, she and her sister helped you, and if it wasn't for them, you would undoubtedly be dead. Their kindness was repaid with Yvonne dying at our hands. Now here we are, sleeping on the ground again and trudging through knee-deep snow that goes on and on as far as we can see. I can't help wondering if leaving in the first place was a good idea. What will we even accomplish? I do not even know how possible it is to complete our task. Don't you think the worlox would have tortured them and killed them by now? It isn't like the demons to take prisoners, let alone keep them alive for any period without reason."

"You want to turn back after we have come so far? Those soldiers were my brothers and sisters in arms. What kind of leader would I be if I abandoned them to their fate?"

"A responsible one that looks at the bigger picture. The wizard order needs you, and for our insubordination, it is likely we will be expelled. The worlox fighting each other leaves them more vulnerable. We should go back to the magister and tell him. The wizard council also needs to know that worlox ash is being sold at the markets. These are things that cannot wait too long. This whole time you haven't said exactly where we are going. I think it is long past due."

"Evera, I told you I am not giving up on them. They would do the same thing for me, they have done the same for me, and I owe each of them my life. I need you to support me in this. We will find them. We have no reason to give up hope."

"Nice deflection, Lorkai. What aren't you telling me?"

Lorkai's eyes narrowed. He paused a second before responding, "I told you everything."

"What do you take me for?" Evera glared.

"You know everything you need to know right now."

"What I *need* to know? I thought we were friends, Lorkai. I thought you could tell me anything."

"There are some things that are best left unsaid for your protection, things that if you knew about, you will be held responsible for. You were right about one thing. There is a bigger picture, but you are missing vital pieces to see the whole picture clearly."

"Do not patronize me! What I do or do not know about this mission that you talked me into is on you. You obviously left out some important details, and since that is the case, you cannot treat me like this. I have never done anything but prove to you I can be trusted. We have been through a lot together, and it hurts knowing you think you can't trust me."

"I didn't say I don't trust you. I want to protect you. Don't you know I would do anything to keep you safe? You are my best friend, like a sister I never had. I would die if anything happened to you because of something I did or said. This is bigger than both of us, and the less you know, the better."

"I'm not a child, Lorkai! When have I ever been someone who needs protecting? Have you suddenly forgotten that we fought together in some battles that both of us barely survived? I know how ruthless the worlox are and what kind of world we live in." Evera abruptly stopped, chewing on the corner of her lip. Then she declared, "I will not go any further with you until you tell me what is going on. I have supported you through all this, even to the point of disobeying the magister and the council because I believe in you. Now it is your turn to trust me."

"Evera, please. You don't know what you are asking!" Lorkai implored.

"Yes, yes, I do, and I am serious. You need to tell me everything right now, or I will turn back."

Sighing, Lorkai looked hard at his feet. "A while back, somewhere around six months ago, me and the wizards who were taken discovered something. In the far north, on a reconnaissance mission, I decided to go with our scouts, figuring they needed all the support they could get. While we skulked around through snowdrifts and ice, we came across a crack in the ground. It was strange. Large rocks were split open as if an axe smote them, and right in the middle of a tundra, this area was completely snowless with a geyser of some green substance flowing from it. Whatever it was, we decided it was a good idea to let it be, but that day we suffered a horrible defeat. One of the wizards suggested we check it out again. He thought that it was a gift and could open the door to a greater power. The rest of us believed he was out of his mind, delusional from all the death and destruction he had seen earlier, but we decided if we went, it would take his mind off the battle. When we arrived, we felt drawn to it, like the stuff spewing forth had a will of its own. Simultaneously, we all stuck our left hands into the geyser without a second thought. The next day, we awoke feeling different. It is hard to describe unless you have experienced it yourself. We were more alert, and the world around us felt raw, like we were newborn babies. Two days later, we were fighting the worlox again, but this time we found that we could do things that we were not able to before. We became faster, our magic more empowered..." Lorkai trailed off, taking in a few slow breaths before continuing. "Like I said, hard to explain if you haven't experienced it before, and you know I am not much of a storyteller. But anyway, what if this geyser is the means to victory? The worlox eventually found out what we discovered, and that is why the wizards are locked up. I was away planning another battle when they attacked. That is how I know the worlox will not kill them. Evera, if we could harness the power we discovered, imagine what that would mean. The worlox would not stand a chance. We could finally have the world all wizards have fought so long for, a world without worlox oppression!"

"Lorkai..."

"This is our chance. We finally can have an edge! With the worlox now fighting each other and this new weapon I discovered, the end of the war is finally in sight."

"Haven't you been paying attention at all?" Evera sighed, shaking her head.

"What?" Lorkai said, throwing his hands upward.

"You literally just saw what such ambitions do to a person. Don't you think Yvonne and May had good intentions too? Don't you think they wanted to help people? Of course they did! Look at what happened, one of them is dead now. Great, you want to end the war.

Every wizard can say the same thing, but what price are you willing to pay?"

"Anything! You should be too! What the wizards have been doing, what we have been doing, is not working. This is why I did not want to tell you. You get scared every time something is suggested that is outside your box of understanding."

"That is not fair. I came with you, didn't I?"

"Yes, and you have been reminding me of it the whole trip," Lorkai glowered.

"Lorkai, I'm glad you told me. Please, I'm not trying to judge you. I am concerned for you. We don't know anything about this geyser that you found or what the results could be of using it, but I agree that all options are worth exploring to give us an edge in the war, as long as it does not cost the best parts of us. If we lose who we are when we fight the worlox, we might as well be another type of demon that fights demons."

Lorkai's stern expression suddenly cracked, half smiling at his friend. "You are always a voice of reason, aren't you?" he chuckled. "Don't worry, I know what I'm doing. I will save Goandria, whatever it takes, but you don't need to worry about me. This is completely different from what those old women were into."

"I hope you're right."

As the two friends argued, brown eyes watched from behind a gray fur hood. A large nose stood out from the blackness within the hood, its nostrils flaring as they puffed out the cold air. Laying on his stomach, he remained utterly still. Several seconds passed. His left hand went for the sword hanging on his right hip as his right hand slowly began to hoist him up, but one of the wizards turned, and the figure collapsed.

Chapter 5

"Snow, as far as the eye can see in all directions, and look more snow is falling!" Lorkai grumbled.

"Not to mention the wind. Ever since we left, I swear it blows harder every day," Evera added.

"Two days we have been freezing out here. At least at the house I was warm, even if our hosts were a little off," Lorkai said.

"All this snow blowing around makes it hard to see. Are you sure we are even going in the right direction anymore?"

"No, not really," Lorkai shouted over the wind.

"Why didn't you say anything?"

"Because we need to keep moving, Evera. What other option do we have? It isn't like we can see well enough to turn back."

"You said the worlox sanctum was about a day's walk. I think you may have misjudged the distance, or we have been lost a lot longer than you realize."

"Probably both." Lorkai shrugged.

"We should probably head deeper into the forest and try to get a fire going," Evera suggested.

"With this wind? We would probably burn the forest down!"

"That is why I thought maybe a little further into the woods would be better. Maybe the trees would offer enough protection to make a fire possible. Hey, if we do burn down the forest, at least we will be warm," Evera chuckled.

"Sadly, that does sound rather tempting. I can't feel my toes or fingers."

"Me either. I hate to say it, but if we continue like this, frostbite is inevitable. You are right, though. This wind is way too strong to build a fire, even in the woods," Evera said, a gust of wind ripping right through her clothes.

"They should have given us thicker cloaks at the temple," Lorkai moaned.

"What do you suggest we do?"

"I really don't know. We are stuck now. The only thing we can do is keep moving. Make sure you move your fingers and toes often to keep the blood flowing," Lorkai answered.

"Hey, do you see that?" Evera pointed eastward from where they were standing. "What is it?"

"I can't tell. Let's head over there. We can't be in any worse of a situation than what we are already in," Lorkai answered.

"I hope you're right," Evera breathed, wrapping her arms as tightly around her as she could.

It was nearly a half-hour later when stone and brick became fully visible through the blowing snow. Elation quickly soured upon the sight. Their skin was blue and purple, and their bodies trembled violently, but what they saw was no comfort. "How? How can it be?" Lorkai collapsed to all fours, no longer caring if the snow stung his hands. Evera remained where she was, looking with sullen eyes at what lay before them.

"After two days! Two days we wandered that stinking wasteland, and we end up right back where we started," Lorkai moaned through clenched teeth.

"Grivear it seems to be our destiny to continually find our way to this village…"

"All that time, Evera, wasted. All the while, our people endure unspeakable torment."

"There is nothing left but to find the inn and warm up. You know we cannot travel any further without rest, food, and a good fire."

Just thirty paces from the market, a log building shaped like a cross with a thatched roof sat at the bottom of three snow-covered hills. Rows of towering pines encompassed the area, save for a narrow path of trampled snow leading to a green door at the front of the structure. A sign partially covered by snow reading "Welcome to the Northland Inn" hung just over the door.

Lorkai smirked, seeing the sign as they drew closer to the inn. "They couldn't have come up with a better name?"

"As long as they have a room open, who cares?" Evera said, rolling her eyes.

Within the inn, a fire burned in a fire place in the back wall, and at the counter, a young red-haired woman rested her chin on her palm. "Welcome to Northland Inn," she said in monotone as the wizards stepped in.

"Hello," Evera greeted far more cheerfully. "Do you have any rooms available?"

"Yep," the red-haired woman said without even looking up.

There was silence for several seconds before Evera spoke up again. "Well?"

"Well what?" the inn keeper asked nonchalantly.

"Our room?" Lorkai said, raising an eyebrow.

"Oh, yes, would you like one room or two?"

"One is fine. I can sleep on the floor," Lorkai said. "As long as I am warm. I can sleep anywhere."

"Yes, one will do fine."

"Okay, then follow me."

The woman slowly walked along to the southeastern portion of the room, unlocking the door they came to. "Here you are," she said, handing Evera the key. "There is a fireplace there, and if you need more wood just come to the front. I have plenty. If you need anything, let me know." Then she turned and walked back to the counter in a daze.

"I seriously doubt she could help us in any fashion," Lorkai shook his head.

"What horrible service!" Evera exclaimed, shutting the door behind her. "But we are warm, and that is what matters."

"Yes, some food and water would be nice, but that would mean having to deal with miss apathetic out there."

"What is going on? This place isn't exactly busy. I would think she would be grateful for the business," Evera said.

In no time, a fire was going in the fireplace, and the two friends huddled around it, hovering their hands over the warmth. Their boots lay close to the flames, and their cloaks were hung to dry. The light of the fire glistened in

Lorkai's eyes as he watched it devour the splintered log. His front teeth chewed the edge of his lip, but the rest of the wizard was still. His mind looped constantly around the reoccurring dream of the wolf and the dark warrior. *Is this my fate? To become this, whatever it is, that I keep seeing? What if it is right? What if the wolf is a reflection of my true being?* His mind relived Yvonne's death over and over. He wanted Evera to believe it was hard, that the old lady had to die out of necessity. Lorkai even tried to convince himself that he hated the whole business, but he knew better. He knew it was as easy as killing a worlox. *Shouldn't I feel something? Guilt? Anger?* He felt nothing, just complete and utter indifference toward the taking of Yvonne's life. In fact, Lorkai did not even feel guilty about not feeling any remorse. He felt like it was a job that needed to be done, nothing more. Lorkai wondered if such absence of guilt was normal. He wondered if he might still be in shock and that might be explanation of his numbness. Again, though, his internal voice called him a liar. He knew that taking another life had been increasingly easy as the war wore on. Whether it was the constant fighting and witnessing several of his fellow wizards die horribly or simply his personality, he did not know.

As Lorkai sat reeling in his thoughts, Evera's mind kept returning to Yvonne's death, but in a far different manner. Her fingers were interlocked, and her hands rested upon her lap, slightly trembling. Everywhere her thoughts went, Yvonne lurked in the background. Evera saw Yvonne's face whether her eyes were open or closed. She saw Yvonne as they passed through the market again. Her heart thumped at a consistent elevated rate, and in spite of her fatigue, sleep was far from possible. While in the wilderness, she put on a smile, joked with Lorkai, and talked to him like nothing was wrong. Internally was a different matter. *How could we let this happen to the poor old women? Maybe we could have helped poor May instead of abandoning her to her grief. All they wanted to do was help us, and one ended up dying. Yvonne may have gone to horrible lengths in her desperation, but I can't criticize her reasons for using the worlox ash. Is this what Goandria has been reduced to? Two sides fighting bitterly over control while the people are ignored?* She sighed mid-thought, and her eyes glanced at Lorkai for a few seconds before returning to the fire. Lorkai's eyes were now shut, and his head tilted down and to the left. "Good, he needs to sleep," Evera said softly as she stood up and climbed into bed herself. As unlikely as sleep was for her that night, she figured it best to try nonetheless.

Two-hours later, Evera's anxieties finally succumbed to the need for sleep. Despite the old building, the air was warm and cozy, much different than the two wizards had been accustomed to over the past couple days. Lorkai awoke with a bit of a start and quickly curled up on the floor beneath a thick wool blanket. Then something caught his ear, *crunch, crunch, crunch,* followed by a series of scratches near the window. *Must be an animal trying to get warm.* Nothing happened for some time, and Lorkai nearly found sleep again when a large rock crashed through the window of their room. Casting aside his blanket and jumping to his feet, Lorkai immediately grabbed his weapon.

"What…"

"Shhh!" Lorkai blurted, silencing Evera before she could say any more.

Lorkai's blood coursed quickly through his veins, his eyes wide as he lay in wait for whatever was to come next. Then, arrow after arrow flew through the broken window. The projectiles thudded into the walls and furniture. One arrow even smashed through an oil lamp, which was fortunately unlit.

"Get down!" Lorkai called out to Evera, but she had already rolled out of bed and sprawled out on the floor.

"Coward! Come and face us instead of hiding like a scared little child!" Lorkai shouted, but the only reply was several more arrow shafts striking the wall.

Lorkai gave a throaty growl. Baring his teeth, he dove through the shattered window. His eyes narrowed as he scanned the darkness for any sort of movement. The sword in his right hand was held high, and its edges burned with a bright red-orange glow. One foot slowly pressed down in front of the other. All the wizard heard was the wind shaking the nearby trees. He stood there, listening, waiting for the assailant to make a mistake and reveal himself. *Phfft, phfft,* two arrows sailed toward Lorkai, striking uselessly against an invisible barrier around him.

"Got you," Lorkai muttered. The wizard charged forward but was met by an explosion of black energy that flung him to his back.

A deep chuckle echoed in the night. "Do you think you are the first wizards I have encountered?"

"Who are you? What do you want from us?"

"To do my job of course. You say I'm a coward, but one does not do this line of work while being stupid."

"What job? What do you want?" Lorkai asked again.

"You still don't know? My, aren't you slow," the voice in the darkness sneered. Then an electrical sphere hit him in the chest.

"Not as slow as you apparently," Evera countered, running up to Lorkai. "Are you alright?"

"Yes, my pride is wounded more." Lorkai wiped the snow off himself.

"Where is he?" Evera asked. "I know I hit him."

"Gone, it would seem. He probably knows he can't take two wizards alone. So on top of everything, we now have a mercenary after us," Lorkai sighed.

"Why?"

"Maybe there is a bounty on all wizards, or maybe someone has it out for just us."

"Who, though, would send a merc after us, and who has that kind of money?" Evera breathed, looking in the depths of the night-shrouded scenery.

"I can think of someone who has more reason than any to hate us."

Chapter 6

Yet another bout of snow swept through northern Goandria, but the following afternoon, the clouds parted, giving way to blue skies and abundant sunshine. Rellin and his brother forged ahead over the western horizon with swarms of worlox behind the shadow lords. Despite the gray and sunless sky, Rellin still covered his eyes, wincing and glowering upward as he moved. *The brightness! The awful brightness of this area! At least there we did not have to contend with the stinking sun,* he thought bitterly.

Memories clawed at his mind. Caves, caverns, tunnels, and stone everywhere. Nothing was smooth or symmetrical, but jagged and rough. The very land itself hungered to tear apart the worlox captives. Darkness, absolute darkness in that ancient realm the worlox lived in long ago. A darkness that hung in the air like fog, with an endless stench of rotting flesh accompanying the black, even though there was nothing living to decay. However black it was, the worlox were not blind, and above in the remote distance there was what may be akin to a sky where the life of Goandria could be seen by a select few. The life of Goandria and the realms of Voshnore sent vibrations through that world, like ripples on a lake, felt by all. Rellin recalled the eons in the dark that sapped all life. He and his kin craved that life but hated it at the same time. Life itself became an embodiment of all the worlox despised. Feeling the beauty of the living seep through to their realm only exacerbated their angry hearts. Hundreds upon hundreds of times, the Citheara met, planning ways to emerge and conquer Goandria, but all failed. That is, until one day, when everything changed, and the worlox were free. Rellin smiled, remembering the first climb out of the fissure onto Goandrian soil. The color, the sounds, and the vibrancy of life were all closer than ever before.

"The poor fools who are still stuck there or were forced to return. They probably wish they could die there. If only I could send Anif back. The smug imbecile, thinking I would ever want to rule side by side with *him*. Like I do not know my brother! He will kill me the first chance he gets, and her too. All he knows is how to care for himself. Family has never meant anything to him before, and now I am supposed to trust him? Look at him. He thinks he has won, that I have fallen for his scheme. I should have killed him long ago. He never did the worlox any good.

"I am the true visionary of the Citheara! If only they would do things my way, it would not have to come to a betrayal. Vox and his sanctimonious attitude! His new way will only make us weak! We allowed the humans to live because they were believed to no longer pose a threat, and now look where we stand! The wizards have continually grown stronger with each passing generation, and all the Citheara propose are passive solutions." Rellin's thoughts were abruptly sidetracked by the southern horizon, which yielded another worlox army. Nearly a mile of land teemed with metal-encrusted soldiers, their mistress at the head. The warlord's four eyes were steely and never shifted direction, resting solely on Anif and Rellin as if she was looking through them.

"Rellin, Anif, it has been awhile. But once serving on the Citheara together does not mean anything. If you dare to march against me, you will be killed like all the others who have tried."

"We don't want to fight you. We have come to join forces with you," Anif said with a slight bow.

The warlord's eyes narrowed even more. "How did you two blundering fools find me?"

"It wasn't that hard. You do have an army following you, after all," Rellin pointed out.

"You say you want to join me?" She said slowly. "You two have always been backstabbing little schemers. The Citheara could have put you up to this, or you really want to join me, then later kill me and take control of the armies yourself."

"Zeneth, come on, is that really how you want to start this discussion? Calling us names? That is a little beneath a warlord, isn't it? Or should I call you a war-lady? How exactly does that work in your case?" Rellin curled the corner of his upper lip as he spat the words at her.

"You confront me with your armies behind you, and say you want to join me. What did you think was going to happen?"

The shadow worlox turned to each other. "We thought there was a chance to join the new order," Rellin said.

"When I was a member of the Citheara, I recall you two did not agree on much. Why this sudden desire to betray the tradition you came from?"

"You are the one who rebelled. It is you who needs all the help you can muster because as we speak, the

Citheara are planning to eliminate you and your army. Who, then, are you to question us and our support when you are the ultimate traitor?" Anif scoffed.

"With you, Zeneth, we see a chance to finally destroy the wizards and to rule our people with the strength they deserve," Rellin added.

For a few seconds, Zeneth merely stared at the brothers, unblinking and unmoving. Then her lips parted slightly. "Countless millennia we were trapped together in that prison. I learned in that time that none of our kind can be trusted, only subdued and dominated. For a time the Citheara filled that role, but no more. I will be the only one that rules the worlox! You shadow worlox are the lowest of our kind, mutants that know nothing of intelligence or true power, but there is something you were not wrong about." A smile suddenly formed on her lips, revealing her sharp yellow and black fangs. "I do need you." She roared, firing an emission of black tendrils that smothered Anif and Rellin.

"No! Ahh, no! You witch!" They screamed and writhed.

"Now, I could have simply obliterated you, but what is the fun in that when you wouldn't suffer?" Zeneth giggled. "I did not get to where I am by trusting. No, I became the most powerful, the most cunning. You two are merely fools with a dream to become like me, but I want you to realize that you have failed! You are nothing!" she shouted, laughing merrily while the living darkness now flowed from both hands.

"Kill… her!" Anif ordered his troops, but nothing happened.

"Your foot soldiers know power when they see it. Even if they did attack, it would be pointless, don't you see? I am not simply killing you. No, that would be such a waste. I am stealing your essence, and I did the same to all the other worlox who took up arms against me. I told you I needed you. Your essence and your armies will serve me well." With one final cackle, she reduced the shadow worlox to ash. Facing the soldiers once under the command of the fallen, she said, "Will you choose to fight with me or to suffer their fate? How loyal are you to your former masters? Will you join me and humble the Citheara?" Hundreds of thousands of knees bent before the warlord.

Zeneth abruptly flared her nostrils, and her mane grew brighter as she inhaled deeply. "I can sense you, kinsmen. You are there, aren't you, Vox? Always spying and ever loyal to the Citheara. Why don't you come out? I could use your power. Imagine how yet another warlord would add to it! You are a slippery one, Vox, but as you see, there are things you did not account for. How long have you been following the snakes? Hmm?" While she spoke, her large but lithe body undulated through the front lines of the newly acquired armies, meticulously scanning each face behind the black helms. "Vox, are you seriously going to make me search every single one of them for you? I know that you can shift your shape and look like one of them, but how well can you hide? How long until I find you and roast you like these two vermin? Even the berserkers are no match for me. What chance, then, do you have? Come, Vox. This is all rather pointless." She allowed some time to pass quietly, still combing through the ranks of worlox infantry. "So, you elect to cower before me. That is a start. Perhaps you are considering offering to join me? As you can see, that is a waste of time. All that are useful to me are these drones we use for infantry. The only chance you have is for a swift death if you step forward now." No one took up the offer, and after searching through three rows of the infantry, Zeneth stormed off screaming, "Fine then play your game!"

When the warlord reached the area where the three armies converged, all demons snapped to attention. Zeneth's head pivoted back and forth. With a soft smile on her face, she raised her hands before her, looking upon the numerous soldiers at her command. "My servants, you have done well to choose the side of victory and power. Those who are new will not regret their decision, for your masters, Anif and Rellin, only saw a small portion of what I have to offer. Their stupidity has opened an advantage for us: two members of the Citheara have been killed, and their armies are now mine. Undoubtedly, the Citheara knows nothing of the traitors in their midst, which is why the time is ripe to attack the Citheara sanctum! We have attacked every army they sent at us and come out victorious with minimal casualties. It is obvious the Citheara are weak. They have grown fat and lazy, and in their moment of desperation, they throw berserkers and spies at us and think we do not know what they have planned!"

Zeneth's four eyes swiveled to the army that once served Rellin. "Do you hear that, Vox? You will join me, willing or not." She giggled like a drunkard. "That is the reality all worlox must realize. The Citheara's hold on our kind is no more, I am the queen of darkness, and all worlox will bow before me. The humans and englifs that infect Goandria will be obliterated, and this world will be made new, in my image! A paradise for all worlox." Once Zeneth finished her ramblings, she drifted through the sea of worlox soldiers to the northeastern rim of the army, and as one, the worlox turned with straight backs to follow their new mistress.

Chapter 7

"It s-s-seems to be our destiny to be s-s-stuck outside in this nasty c-c-cold, in this nasty little village, in this nasty little c-c-corner of the world," Lorkai whined through chattering teeth.

"C-c-can't we build a bigger fire?"

"And have that mercenary find us?" Lorkai retorted.

"I'm not gunna s-s-sit here and sh-sh-shiver all night," Evera said, standing up and dusting the snow off her robes.

"Wait! Where are you going?"

"Back to the inn! I'm not freezing out here any longer!" Evera snapped.

"He'll find you!"

"I'm not going alone," Evera commanded.

"If we go back, we are vulnerable again," Lorkai pleaded.

"We are vulnerable if we s-s-stay out here!"

The walk back to the inn was about ten minutes, but with each movement of her legs, Evera's knees reluctantly bent. She hadn't been able to feel her toes in well over an hour, and her fingers hardly moved when she wanted them to. "If he thinks I'm going to spend another night freezing when there is a perfectly warm inn right over there, he is a fool. If the merc comes again, we will deal with it. We are wizards! Why is Lorkai insisting we hide? He is usually the one looking to pick a fight! We have been friends for years, and sometimes I still do not understand him," Evera mumbled to herself. After the final words left her mouth, Lorkai's footsteps reminded her of his presence. Glancing over her right shoulder, Evera saw he was merely two or three paces behind her. Her face became flushed. If he heard her, which she believed he had, Lorkai never let on.

Soon the wizards found themselves back at the inn. The snow glistened in the moonlight like minuscule diamonds, illuminating the woodland with a soft white glow. Upon entering the inn, Evera hurried to the fireplace. "I'm so tired of this never-ending cold that permeates this region!" she complained, rubbing her palms together over the fire.

"Where is the inn keeper?" Lorkai asked abruptly, completely ignoring his friend's comment.

"Why does it matter? She's not totally there anyway."

"Well, considering we never officially checked out and now the window is broken, we should probably let her know."

"All I care about is getting warm right now. The rest can wait," Evera said.

"That much is clear, Evera, but we need a plan moving forward here. Someone is after us, and we need to get to the bottom of it."

"Why? You said yourself he was obviously hired by May. She is an old, grieving lady. Do you propose we kill her too?"

Lorkai glared at Evera. "That's a low blow. Why don't you just come out and say it? You don't think I should have killed Yvonne. You think that somehow there was another way. Your passive-aggressive comments are telling, Evera. I have already explained myself. You say you understand, yet your comments persist. Why don't you just get it off your chest and tell me how you feel?"

"How I really feel is that you have been acting strange. There has been something bothering you. I can see it, but you won't tell me what it is. You only just recently told me where we were going and why saving your friends is so important. I want you to let me in, but for some reason you don't trust me. Then there is this business of hiding outside from a single mercenary. We are wizards, Lorkai. Why should we hide from him? He took us by surprise once, and he is cunning, but that is no reason to hide when we still have the upper hand!"

"He could have killed you, Evera! I am not going to have either of us get killed by a sword-for-hire. We are not cowering to him; we are picking our battles and staying on task. And something else, just because you are my friend does not mean you are entitled to know my business. I told you before that I want to keep you safe."

"Lorkai, I'm not some helpless peasant who hasn't held a weapon before! I am a wizard!"

Lorkai sighed, shook his head, and bit his lower lip. "Evera, you were in the temples studying scrolls for a long time. The fact that you are here is on me. Our friendship is the reason you are here."

Evera's lips formed a smile, and her eyes softened as they met Lorkai's. "I already told you, you need to stop worrying about me."

"I can't, Evera. What if we let our guard down and that mercenary manages to kill you?"

"He won't."

"What if?"

"He won't," Evera calmly repeated.

"How about you just get some rest, and I will keep watch?" Lorkai suggested.

"But what about you? You need to sleep too."

"If we are going to stay here, then I would feel better if I kept watch."

"It is going to be cold in our room with the window broken," Evera said.

"Just sleep out here. When the inn keeper comes back, I will let her know what happened."

Evera was soon fast asleep on the floor in front of the fire. Lorkai sat with his knees against his chest across from the lobby window. His right hand gripped the pommel of his sword tightly as he stared out into the nothingness behind the glass. The wizard expected to see more arrows zip through the window or a shape dart across the viewing area of the window. But nothing happened. For what seemed like days to the wizard, he sat there, not moving except to continually chew on his lower lip. Eventually the inn keeper flung open the door, stamped her feet, and hung up her coat on a nearby hook.

"Oh! You startled me!" Her gasp was followed by a lighthearted chuckle.

"And you don't seem totally out of it," Lorkai said, raising his right eyebrow. He then realized what had just come out of his mouth.

"Huh?" She said, tilting her head.

"Never mind."

"Were you looking for a room?"

"No, no, we already have one. I wanted to tell you that someone threw a rock through our window and attacked us. Needless to say, we are not able to sleep in there tonight."

"You checked in already?"

Lorkai sighed and pursed his lips together. "Yes, you did it yourself."

"Hmm, you were attacked, you say? How curious. Are you two alright?"

"Yes, we are. Thank you. You didn't hear the glass shattering or the barrage of arrows hitting the wall?"

"No, I had some… errands to run," the inn keeper responded hesitantly.

"I sleep in the room next to yours. You and your friend are more than welcome to sleep out here if it suits you, but I'm going to turn in for the night. Let me know if you need anything."

"We will. Thank you."

So strange. It is like she is a completely different person. Is she overly fond of the drink? Maybe she suffers from some mental illness? There is something not right here. Lorkai thought. His eyes slowly moved upward. *Are you testing me? Did you bring me back here for a reason? Whenever I've had this feeling, it was for a reason. What are you trying to tell me? It feels like this town is sick. After spending two days in the freezing cold and trying to get to the sanctum as quickly as possible, we end up back here. Is this you guiding us? I don't know. Maybe we are just a couple of hapless fools on a hopeless crusade.*

Dawn came. The new rays of light offered a strange new hope, for no more attacks came that night. Lorkai breathed more deeply. His eyelids felt heavy as he turned to see his friend waking up. Smiling, he thought, *Good, she got more rest than I figured she would.* That was the last moment Lorkai could recall before suddenly feeling nudged and hearing his name being called out.

"Mmm, what?" he moaned, his eyes refusing to open, for they wanted only to lead him back to slumber.

"I know you need to rest, but it is nearly mid-day, and I know you wouldn't want me to let you sleep that long."

"Oh, yes I do," he said, turning over. Then a few seconds later his eyes popped open. "Nearly mid-day! You can't be serious!"

"~~Yeah,~~ I left you here and bought us some warmer cloaks. These are made of thick wool and much better suited for the weather. I probably should have gotten them sooner," Evera said, tossing the new cloak to Lorkai.

"These should definitely help."

"I also managed to buy a map while I was at the market. I'm not very interested in getting lost again," Evera said.

"You are really on top of things today, aren't you?"

"I guess you could say that. There is more."

"Like what? You bought enough food to last us the rest of the journey?" Lorkai perked up.

"Not exactly. I decided to do some digging into this mystery of the worlox ashes. We are here anyway, and we might as well try to find out how far the problem has spread."

Lorkai slumped a little. "I wondered how long it would take before you did something like that, but to be honest with you, I thought about doing it myself." Lorkai paused, scanned the area, then continued, "When the inn keeper returned last night, she was totally different. It was as if she had been possessed before. She seemed alert and friendly this time instead of cold and distant. She also did not seem to have any recollection of us. I cannot shake this feeling that there is more going on here than we can see. Maybe there is something else going on that is connected to the worlox ash we found at May's house and the mercenary who attacked us."

"I think you are right. There may be a connection," Evera said, pacing as she spoke. "See, I did some asking around, and apparently one of the merchants sells the ash on the side."

"Did you find out which one?" Lorkai interjected.

"No, not really, outside of a few suspicious characters, but let's face it, that is pretty much everyone in town. Here is the interesting part: I figured the merchant wasn't obtaining the ash himself but instead purchasing from someone else. Who that person is, I am still not sure, but who would make the most profit from selling contraband from the battlefield? Mercenaries!"

"So you think that is the connection? He might not have been hired by May after all. He may fear his business might go under if the rest of our order finds out what he is up to. That would make sense, except how would he know we know unless May tipped him off out of revenge?"

"That is possible, too. I didn't really feel right about leaving here in the first place, and now that we are back, I feel like it is for a reason. We need to help these people and show them that the wizards still care about the people."

"I know, and you are right about that point, but that does not resolve the issue of why we set out in the first place. We meant to simply pass through here, not to stay for any length of time. The truth is, in a war such as this, the people will suffer. It is inevitable but sometimes necessary. We cannot stop what we are doing to help these tiny villages. The wizards are spread thin as it is, and there is one thing you seem to be forgetting: I am still the general of the wizard armies. They will need me to return as soon as possible. I'm torn too, but I still feel like we cannot delay any longer here."

"Then what do you suggest, Lorkai? I am not going to just ignore the problem here anymore."

"If that is how you feel, I won't stop you, but as much as I agree this is a problem that needs to be addressed, we do not have the time to spend. If you really want to help these people, then you can stay while I continue the mission."

"Lorkai…"

The wizard raised his hand, stopping Evera mid-sentence. "This is the best option. You need to uncover just how deep the problem of using the worlox ash runs and the effects it has on the people. Splitting up also keeps both of our consciences clear."

"Just give me a few days, Lorkai. You will need me out there. This is too big of a job for the two of us, let alone you going in by yourself. It's suicide going into a worlox sanctum alone. I don't like this, Lorkai. I don't like it at all."

Lorkai took Evera's hand, and his eyes met hers. "You know this is for the best, though."

"What if the mercenary finds you while you are sleeping?"

"I can handle him. As you said, we are wizards after all." Lorkai winked.

Goandria: The Schism

Part III

Chapter 1

The ground shook, and light flashed in the distance. Rumblings echoed across the barren land, like a giant hammer striking an anvil. Any observer would think a terrible storm was brewing in the south, but this was not just a storm. Blackness overcame the white-covered landscape – a mechanized black of metal and otherworldly powers. Animals scurried away in terror for miles around, giving the demons ample leeway. As the worlox army swallowed up miles of territory, the sky also darkened. Violet lightning arched along the heavens, as if the sky itself was shattering. One bolt of lightning struck the fortress in front of the massive army. Zeneth smiled, seeing the stone crumble away and smash down on top of the sentries below. Thick, black, smoke-like material streamed skyward from the citadel, completely shrouding the rest of the sky. From within the keep, black, winged creatures rimmed with blue fire leapt forth. High-pitched screeches rang out from the beings, clawing and snarling as they advanced on Zeneth's forces.

"Is this all the Citheara can throw at me? Where are your mighty armies now? Who will save you from me, the goddess of the worlox?" Zeneth snarled under her breath. Immediately after she spoke, a loud thud came from the gate followed by *ting, ting, ting*. The huge iron barrier slowly rose. Dozens of berserker worlox came forth from the gateway. Dozens soon turned to hundreds, and hundreds became thousands of the blue, fiery demons. Another gate on the western side of the sanctum also opened, pouring out the massive infantry in service to the Citheara.

"Ooh, they look threatened. Bringing out the berserkers makes them look like they are trying to compensate for their inadequate power." Zeneth chuckled. All but the soldiers closest to the warlord remained completely still. Those at Zeneth's side hastily glanced at her. At first, their mistress simply ignored them, but as the seconds passed, she turned to one and said in a very calm and soft voice, "You will hold."

No one replied, for no one dared to, but the enemy was advancing quickly, and orders had yet to be given. Zeneth casually stepped forward as the Citheara's armies halted their advance before her. The winged worlox snarled and chomped as they flew overhead like vultures. The berserkers beat their war hammers against the ground, challenging Zeneth to make the first move.

"Servants of the Citheara, you have a choice today. The same choice that was given to those who now follow me will be given to you. You can join me and destroy your former masters, making history and allying with the most powerful worlox goddess to exist, or you will die this day. I have absorbed the power of every one of our kind that has challenged me. I am more powerful than any worlox, and even Voshnore himself. If you join me, we will not simply have victory over Goandria, but over Voshnore's realm as well!" Zeneth waited for some time, but no one stepped over to her side, not even a single infantryman. Her eyes slowly looked over the army before her, her nostrils flaring. "So you willingly choose to die, willingly choose to slap away the opportunity for greatness I present to you?"

"That is because they know you are insane, Zeneth," a scratchy voice called from the summit of the citadel. All eyes shifted toward the source of the voice. It was another warlord. His mane flared as he gazed down upon the armies. Even as far up as he was, he seemed large. His feet nearly took up the entire space on the citadel's summit, and his clawed toes wrapped around the edge like a bird of prey. "They know you can't offer anything. You are a traitor, and you know how the Citheara deal with traitors, but such a fate is too good for you. You will be defeated, and your armies will be shown no mercy for siding with you. But you, Zeneth, we have something special in store for you." Without saying any more, the demon turned his back, and the winged demons instantly descended upon Zeneth's armies. As soon as their allies began their assault from above, the berserkers stomped forward, their war hammers reducing scores of Zeneth's infantry to ashes.

Through the battle, Zeneth kept still, watching idly as her soldiers were being killed. Her face beamed with a large, toothy grin. Laughing hysterically, she unleashed her weapon. The worlox in service of Zeneth paused for just a second, for they knew what was coming. Electrified coils of blackness flowed from Zeneth's fingers, engulfing the enemy worlox. "Did I not warn you? Did I not say I am now a goddess? How dare you threaten your new mistress! It is you who will know death!" She squealed while her magic eviscerated her foes. "Who can stand against my might? I am the queen of darkness."

Zeneth turned the tide in her favor. In minutes, thousands of worlox were defeated, and the berserkers were now halved. The warlord perched on the citadel continued to watch, unmoving. After watching the battle for a while, he turned his attention to the east. Mere minutes later, the first wave of worlox soldiers under his command was utterly decimated by Zeneth.

"Charos, you have been defeated. I have become more powerful than any worlox. Join me, your rightful queen, and I will forgive this indiscretion."

Charos gave a deep laugh. "Oh, Zeneth!" he said, then he laughed even more. "You have won nothing, and I have lost nothing."

"Your soldiers have been destroyed, you insolent fool!" Zeneth cried in confusion.

"Fodder, nothing more." Charos waved. With that, an army of shadow worlox materialized along the sanctum's wall. They, like Rellin, were made up of a smoke-like mist. The shadows appeared in mostly-humanoid form, but some had outlines of wings, crowns of horns, or even four to eight arms. It was difficult to tell how many there were, for their forms were not definite, and some chose to appear simply as smoky blobs. Just as the shadow worlox materialized, so too did their weapons; bows comprised of the same smoky material manifested before them, and long black arrows appeared as the strings were drawn.

Zeneth's eyes flashed wide for a moment, and she took a couple steps back, but then she stopped and puffed out her chest. "This still is no match for my power," she uttered. Her fingers rolled into a fist, and she loosed a sharp hiss. This was followed by hundreds of black arrows sailing through the air toward her armies. Five arrows pierced her chest, knocking the usurper backwards. She huffed and panted while her hands each clutched an arrow shaft. A bright orange-red ooze bubbled out of her wounds, soaking the ground around her and scorching the grass. A limitless amount of black arrows pelted the worlox army on the ground, leaving only ash and the remains of plate armor in their wake. Those who were not killed by the shadow archers fled upon seeing Zeneth's defeat. In little time, Zeneth's army had been reduced to less than a quarter of its original size. Once more, the gates of the sanctum were hoisted up, and more infantrymen poured out, outnumbering Zeneth's forces one hundred to one.

Trailing behind the gigantic army, Charos came to Zeneth. His face seemed frozen as he looked upon his enemy. In his left hand, he had a long broadsword. It was black like all worlox weapons. For several minutes, Charos simply gazed upon his foe. Then he placed his foot on her chest, breaking two of the arrow shafts off, and as she howled in agony, he said, "You dare to think you are superior to the Citheara? There will never be one ruler of the worlox. You, Zeneth, are not the first to try, and in attacking so prematurely, you handicapped yourself. If only you had waited and continued to gather your strength, things might have been different, but we both know you are not good with that patience. We of the Citheara thought we had a punishment in mind for you, but I think we will have to revisit that decision, or at least postpone it. I can think of nothing better than to…"

An explosion slammed into Charos' chest, and Zeneth swiped her feet under his, knocking him down as well.

"The problem," Zeneth said as she began slowly getting to her feet, "is that you members of the Citheara think too small. Attacking the sanctum was not premature at all, but a diversion. You have valuable prisoners here with valuable information." Then she hovered her hand over the arrows, causing them to disappear. "You have not won, Charos, because you cannot defeat me." She launched an array of darkness at the other warlord, obliterating him.

Chapter 2

"What have I gotten myself into? Back in the frozen wasteland. Maybe I shouldn't have left Evera in Grivear. Ugh, and I left the map with her! At least she is warm—well, warmer—and I would definitely take warmer right about now. I wonder how long I have been out here," Lorkai grumbled, trudging onward through the ever-deepening snow. *It looks different than the last time Evera and I tried to come this way. There are far fewer trees, and there is definitely more snow. I hope that is a good sign. I should be heading the right way, but last time I thought the same thing. The sun is out, though, and the wind is not gale-force. Actually, if it wasn't for the blistering cold, it would be a pleasant day.*

Lumbering through the knee-high snow caused his joints to burn and beg the wizard for some respite. The muscles in his legs felt tense and hot, but Lorkai still continued. After nearly an hour, his lower body was in utter agony. Falling to his knees, he looked around for any sign that he was closer to his destination, but all he could see was white for miles and miles, with a few scattered pines. He pawed as much snow as possible away from where he stood so he could sit somewhat comfortably. Sitting with his knees slightly bent, resting his chin against his left palm, he realized how completely exhausted he had become. "I will just take a quick rest, but I will soon need to get moving again," he said to himself. He stuffed a few handfuls of snow in his mouth.

The next thing Lorkai knew, he was waking up with cold steel pressed against his neck. "Don't move," a familiar voice demanded. Lorkai's eyes opened slowly, and his hands instinctively went to rub them. "I said don't move, wizard," the voice said again, digging the blade a little further into Lorkai's flesh.

"So you managed to track down a wizard without him noticing? Very impressive, mercenary. I have to say, though, this is not entirely unexpected."

"Let me see your hands!" the mercenary barked, pulling out a piece of rope.

"I thought you were paid to kill me." Lorkai smirked as his hands were bound.

"Quiet!"

"So, if you are going to kill me, why bother tying my hands? Are you lonely out here? Would you like some company until you get to the next settlement where you can fulfill your duty?"

"I get paid whether you are dead or alive, and if you keep talking, you won't be alive."

"What changed? You tried so hard for dead before. If it was dead or alive, all you had to do was ask nicely."

"Do you think being smart with me is wise?" the mercenary challenged.

"Do you think this will actually go well for you? Walk away while you still can. Go home to your friends and family, if you have any, and forget about this job. I can promise you that you will not get paid, and I am not going with you."

"Bold words for one in your position. You are a wizard, not a god. Now get up slowly."

"You really do not want to do this. If you really have fought wizards before, you would know this is not a good idea."

"Be quiet or lose your tongue!"

"It should not surprise you that I am not going anywhere with you. I don't think you are actually willing to kill me. Sure, you put on a good show in Grivear, but I see it now. Your eyes tell me you really do not want to do this job, that you are scared of me," Lorkai continued to press.

"Is that so?" The mercenary raised his sword and pressed it even harder against Lorkai, causing a trickle of blood to run down the wizard's neck.

"Well, here is your chance. You will not get another opportunity. Kill me and get your bounty because, like I said, I am not going anywhere with you."

The mercenary slightly lowered his sword, eyed the ground, then turned his lips inward, and put his weapon back against Lorkai's neck. "No, you will come with me or die. It's that simple."

With nearly-inhuman reflexes, Lorkai rammed his head into the merc and hit him with a surge of green lightning from his palms. The attack not only shocked the mercenary, but also burned through the rope that bound Lorkai's hands. Lorkai now stood over the other, his sword tip digging into the mercenary's neck.

"Another mistake you made: you did not take my weapon. You should have taken your chance while you had it. I can live with attempting to hurt me. You are not the first and undoubtedly not the last. But scaring my friend and coming after her is not something I can forgive. Now, you are going to tell me everything that is going on. Why are you after us, who hired you, and what is going on in Grivear?"

The hired sword swallowed hard and flared his nostrils in defiance.

"Stubborn to the very end, I see." Lorkai sneered, punching the other man in the face. The wizard's sword glowed bright red-orange, his grasp so firm around the hilt his knuckles turned white. "I am not going to ask again. That is a promise."

"Alright, alright!" the mercenary whined at last, raising his hands in defeat. "You win. I did not really want to take this job, but the money is good."

"Keep going," Lorkai ordered.

"I typically don't take jobs that may potentially require actual fighting. As I said before, I have faced other members of your order in the past. I thought I was prepared this time, but I clearly wasn't.

"There's a produce merchant, goes by Wolt. He hired several mercenaries to comb the battlefields for worlox ash. It used to be pretty rare to find, but it seems you wizards have gotten more diligent lately. There have been piles of the stuff pretty much everywhere, even in places I didn't think the worlox were anymore."

"So Evera was right," Lorkai said under his breath. "How widespread is the problem?"

"I don't know. I just gather what I can and sell it, but now that it has become more common, the price has fallen, and I have to bring back four times as much just to make a living."

"Your livelihood is of no concern to me. I asked how big the problem is." Lorkai lowered his voice.

The merc glowered at Lorkai for a few seconds. "I told you, I don't know."

"I don't believe you. I think you at least have an idea because you know how much and for how long you have been doing this, and you know it is illegal. Of course, that is what your kind does. Break the laws to make a little money, no matter whose lives are ruined."

"You wizards are all the same. Sanctimonious hypocrites," the merc spat.

"Says the lowly mercenary who tries to kill his prey while they are sleeping," Lorkai countered. "Was this Wolt guy the one who hired you?"

"For what? To kill you? Yes, he got tipped off that a couple of wizards knew about the ash and figured it was only a matter of time before it was traced back to him and you shut him down or arrested him."

"So you were hired to kill us? Why did you say dead or alive then?" Lorkai asked.

The mercenary was quiet again, resulting in yet another punch to the jaw. He spat out a mouthful of blood and continued to stubbornly glower at the wizard.

"You know what I think? You don't have the stomach for killing. You were hired to kill us, but after you tried, your conscience got the best of you and you decided to lead at least one of us away from Grivear. When I look at you now, I can't believe I ever feared for my friend's safety. You are a coward."

"What do you know about anything, wizard? You know nothing of the troubles in the world. Your kind is just a bunch of religious freaks who fight wars and return to luxury, claiming the whole while that you have a divine gift. While you are warmongering and lounging around, everyone else has to work for a living."

"You echo the words of someone else I met," Lorkai uttered. "But you are in no position to judge anyone, mercenary. How many lives have you ruined by selling the ash?"

"Not nearly as many as any wizard has. The war you have raged with the worlox has cost countless lives, and for what? Centuries later, you are no closer to victory. When are you going to understand that this is the way the world is now? The worlox won. It's time the wizards accept that fact and focus on the people's needs."

"The worlox nearly eradicated everyone. They take slaves at will! Waging a war against them is the only thing that makes sense. It's easy for a coward to critique others when he doesn't get his hands dirty." Lorkai cracked.

"Of course you see it that way. You were trained and indoctrinated to believe a certain way."

"That is an overly-simplistic view that does not require much intellectual thought," Lorkai countered.

Silence ensued, and tension hung in the air before the merc asked, "So what now?"

"Honestly, there are many things I would like to do, but there is only one that is practical. Being a mercenary, I'm guessing you have traveled these parts several times. While I have been here before, nothing looks familiar to me right now. I am on my way to the worlox sanctum, and you are going to help me get there."

"You're crazy! Why would anyone want to go there?"

"That isn't important to you. All you need to concern yourself with is getting us there safely. If you do that, you may be able to keep your life," Lorkai said.

"Why ask all those questions about Grivear if you are not even going back?" the mercenary complained.

"Because I fully intend to go back once I finish with something else. For now, my friend will have to investigate the problem on her own."

"But going to the sanctum is suicide. If you want to kill me, have some honor and do it outright."

"You are the last one to lecture about honor, mercenary. Now get going. We have a long way to go." Lorkai sheathed his weapon and bent over to pick up his cloak.

Just then, a dagger zinged by, barely nicking his face, and the mercenary was on top of the wizard. "You're never taking me to that place!" he wailed, wrapping his hands around Lorkai's throat. Despite the pain in his legs, Lorkai was able to kick the mercenary a couple times, which loosened him just enough for the wizard to punch his assailant in the ribs.

"Try that again, and you will die," Lorkai warned. "Now as I said, we have a long way to go, and you are going to get us to that sanctum."

Chapter 3

The next day seemed like Voshnore was playing a joke, for suddenly the weather was much warmer, and both mercenary and wizard found themselves sweating underneath their winter cloaks. The sun shone brightly for a few hours before gray overtook the sky again, leaving a dense layer of fog over the melting snow. Certain areas of the land had huge puddles forming, resulting in them having to sometimes travel a mile or two out of their way. "I have never seen this kind of weather this far north before," the mercenary said, but the only reply was the tip of a sword biting just a little deeper into his back.

"Be quiet and keep going," Lorkai barked. "How much farther? I don't remember it taking this long."

"I don't know. Probably a few hours, but not any longer. I promise," the merc said with a slight hiss.

"You had better not be stalling," Lorkai threatened.

Neither one said anything more. Lorkai wore a hardened expression, his steely eyes ever upon his captive. "I can't stand to even look at that filth. A hired sword thinking he can lecture me on the ways of the world. He has such insolence, such hypocrisy, that he practically sweats the stuff. He thinks he can condemn *me*? He is the one who tried to kill two people while they were sleeping. Coward." Lorkai's hand balled into a tight fist and his jaw clenched. "I wish I could kill him. If only…"

Three hours passed, and there was still no sign of their destination. All they saw before them was slushy snow, trees, and periodic patches of grass. Lorkai let out a sigh that sounded more like a snarl. "Look, the sun is nearly setting. According to you, we should have been there by now, so you are either lying or stalling."

"No, I'm not! It's all this water we have to go around. There is so much of it, and it's so deep. Even so, we should have at least seen the sanctum by now. Something is not right," the merc replied.

"The agreement was you get me to the sanctum and I might let you live, and you have not kept up your end."

"No, wait, wait!"

Lorkai bit his lower lip. His sword was raised, but it did not make the killing strike. He wanted to kill this man for what he had done to him and Evera, but something stirred within him. In the briefest of moments, the words of the specter wolf that had haunted so many of his dreams came to mind. He saw what he was capable of doing. Lorkai knew it would be easy to kill this man, and he probably deserved it, but he questioned if he was like this mercenary. He felt hatred for this man so deep—it was all he had thought about since they began looking for the sanctum—yet in just a few seconds, he saw what that bitterness was doing to him. Lorkai slowly lowered his weapon, his expression softening. He looked upon the mercenary with wonder instead of contempt for the very first time.

"Are you sure we are in the right area?" Lorkai said more calmly than he expected.

"Yes! I don't understand. We should at least be able to see it." The mercenary whimpered rather pathetically.

"Don't worry. I believe you," Lorkai said, placing his weapon in its scabbard for the first time since they had begun their search. "What is your name?" the wizard suddenly asked. "If we are going to be around each other, we should probably call one another by name."

"We've managed this long. I don't think exchanging names will really make any difference. Let's just find that sanctum, ~~okay~~ alright?"

"So you just want to be called mercenary?" Lorkai's eyebrow rose.

"We aren't friends, wizard. You made that very clear, and don't think because you just had a moment of humanity that I will forget that you threatened my life. Even if I fulfill my part of the deal, you still might kill me. You were right. I should have killed you when I had the chance. The only good wizard is a dead wizard," the merc spat.

Lorkai's jaw tightened again. "Obstinate fool! You are right, we did make a deal, and you still haven't gotten us to the sanctum."

"I already said I can't get you there. It is hidden or something. If that means you are going to kill me, get it over with already."

"So if it was hidden, where would you say it is?" asked Lorkai.

"It should be right there, about five miles northeast."

"Then we head there, whether we see it or not."

As the wizard and mercenary moved onward, more trees enveloped the land. In less than a mile, they found themselves surrounded by rows of pines over one hundred feet tall and three to six feet in diameter. After an hour had passed, the mercenary stopped. "Right here.

It should be right here. I know it, but the sanctum isn't here. I just don't understand. Fortresses just do not disappear."

"Hmm, maybe they do," Lorkai said, slowly closing his eyes and reaching out his left hand. "Yes, I can feel it now. Why didn't I think of this before? Maybe you aren't as incompetent as I thought."

"What? What is it?" the mercenary asked.

Lorkai ignored the question and began advancing into an icy clearing. "Something's different here. Whatever it is, it pulsates with darkness."

"Magic?"

"You might say that, for lack of a better word," Lorkai said.

"Can you do anything about it?"

"I can try, but there are no guarantees. I don't know exactly what we are dealing with."

"You're a wizard, though; sorcery is your specialty," the merc remarked.

"Wizards are not sorcerers. There is a huge difference. Now if you will let me be, I need to concentrate." Lorkai spread his hands out before him, uttering some words that the other man couldn't understand over and over for several minutes. Then he stopped. Nothing happened. Lorkai gritted his teeth, stretched out his hands just a little further and repeated the process. Again nothing happened. Lorkai exhaled deeply and withdrew his sword, thrusting it skyward. The blade of the weapon blazed like brilliant fire. Ever so slightly, rock and stone walls began to materialize piece by piece, but after a few moments, they completely disappeared again. Lorkai repeated the process one more time, and again the structure started to become visible. After a quarter of the sanctum had appeared, an invisible force exploded from the building, stripping the nearby trees of their snow.

An octagonal wall surrounded a taller wall of the same shape, both enclosing around a tall, slender, stone citadel. There were only five small windows visible, but no light came from within the building. All was quiet. No guards were at the gate, and no sentries stood along the wall. Lorkai remained still, taking in the sight of the massive frozen fortress. "I have never seen one of their sanctums in the daylight," he uttered, slowly approaching the structure. As the men drew closer, they saw four shorter towers within the walls. These smaller towers, which had not been visible before, were carved from black stone, and each was connected to the citadel by flying buttresses of the same black material, but they were adorned with silver runes.

They were a few hundred yards from the gate when the mercenary blurted out, "Your kind must have attacked." Lorkai shifted his gaze from the awesome building before him to his immediate surroundings. His feet stopped, and his jaw dropped. Tens of thousands of worlox remains lay sprawled out before the sanctum.

"No, it wasn't the wizards. I only see fallen worlox."

"Then what happened?"

"The worlox. My friend and I saw them fighting one another a couple weeks ago. It seems, though, that no one won this battle."

"Well, I got you here. My part of our deal is fulfilled," the mercenary said, gawking wide-eyed at all the fallen worlox around him. He started to slowly move backward.

Lorkai made eye contact with the other, chewed the corner of his lower lip, and then said, "Indeed you did, but I don't trust you. I told you I *might* let you live."

"You can't be serious!" the mercenary raged.

"You tried to kill me and my friend. That is an indiscretion I cannot take lightly. What if I let you go and you try it again? Or what if you decide to harvest all this worlox ash and help perpetuate the cycle of addiction in Grivear? I think for now it is best you stay here with me."

"No!" the merc shouted, unsheathing his own sword. "I am not going in there, even if that means you strike me dead where I stand. I have done what I needed to do, and I have gone far enough!"

"You don't want to fight me. Put your sword down," Lorkai said.

"I will not! You should have taken it from me when you could."

"I didn't take it from you because even with your weapon, you are no threat to me. Now be reasonable and put down your sword."

"You force me to bring you here, and then you ask me to be reasonable? I will not back down again. Either we go our separate ways, or we fight, here and now."

"Seriously, you don't want to do this. Put down the sword." Lorkai lowered his voice. "I will not ask again."

"Yes, I think I do. There are things that I do not want to see, and the hell that awaits within that sanctum is one of them. I have heard stories. I know what goes on in places like this. The worlox are demons, and you want me to go with you into their home?"

"If you do this, you will force me to kill you," Lorkai said menacingly.

"Fine. I would rather die," the mercenary said, raising his weapon.

Lorkai eyed him. The challenge tempted him. He remembered the hateful things he told himself about this man, but in that moment he saw a man of conviction. Maybe he was a coward, maybe he chose a dishonorable profession, but he was doing what he thought was right and just trying to survive in the world. Here was Lorkai's chance to finally take his revenge, to punish him for what he did, but a feeling deep within his heart stopped him. His mind's eye saw Evera's smile. He heard her voice, as if she was standing right beside him, say, *Lorkai, this isn't right. If you kill him, you are worse than he is. There is no justice in this.* Lorkai lowered his sword and whispered, "Go."

Chapter 4

Evera's hazel eyes peeked out from behind a mound of snow and bushes. She stayed as still as she possibly could, but her legs began to feel tingly after hours of kneeling. Sighing loudly, she resituated so that she could stretch out her legs. She held her neck and rotated her head a few times, resulting in several crackling pops. *A day and a half and nothing,* she thought. *Maybe I should have just gone with Lorkai. What was I thinking? This is a job far too big for one wizard. I hardly know where to begin this investigation. I'm a scholar, not an investigator. I wonder how Lorkai is doing. I sure hope he is having better luck than I am. Well, either way, I'm sure he could use my help right now.* She folded her arms close to her chest and let her imagination run with visions of Lorkai surrounded by demons, imprisoned, or even tortured.

Oh, Lorkai, how I wish I could help you. I just don't know what is wise. I want to help these people, but I also want to be there for you. Even you saw that something must be done about this problem, but can I do it? Voshnore, I need your guidance. Give me strength, give me hope, and give me wisdom! You created the wizard order to protect and love the people, but we have failed in our mission. We have become consumed with war, neglecting our responsibility to the people. The englifs have mostly left the mainland and fortified Caldaria, and few humans remain that are not wizards. My heart just breaks. There are so many to love, so many who need help, and I can't just ignore that. Her hands closed tightly into fists. *We cannot ignore them anymore. The people have lost faith, and if I can do anything to restore that, I will. I don't know where to go. I don't know what to do from here. I feel like a candle in utter darkness that wants to bring fire to the room but can only remain a small flame.*

Evera took in another breath of cool air and resumed watching the market. *This is still probably the best way to get answers, but it's so boring...* Then something, or rather someone, familiar caught her eye. "May?" she whispered, straining her eyes to get a better look. Walking hunched over, Evera quickly shuffled to a nearby snowdrift that was closer to the market. Peeking from the left end of the drift, she saw May talking with a merchant, but it was a different one than she normally was seen doing business with. "Ugh, I can't see," Evera moaned under her breath, dashing toward another pile of snow. *Hmm, I can't tell what she is buying. Of course, I couldn't tell when we were staying with her, either. I feel like a thief stalking the poor woman so I can rob her. This is so ridiculous!* She let out a particularly long sigh. *I guess the best way I can think of to get more information is to find the dealer and question him. No, she definitely isn't buying ash, but I suppose she has enough stockpiled that she wouldn't need to buy more for a while. Who knows, she might have gotten it somewhere else or a long time ago.* While Evera was consumed in her thoughts, she felt a small tap on her right shoulder.

"Whatcha doing?" a small voice asked.

Evera's heart nearly stopped as she quickly turned around to see a small boy mere inches from her face. Clutching her chest, she gasped. "You shouldn't sneak up on people like that!"

The boy, who was probably somewhere between four and five, said nothing. He merely stared at the wizard with a blank expression on his face.

"What are you doing out here all by yourself? Where are your parents?"

The boy shrugged and pointed toward the market. "Are you a bandit? You look too pretty to be a bandit, but my dad says you can't judge what a person is just by looks."

Evera would have giggled under any other circumstance, but the fear of being spotted was ever-present in the back of her mind. "No, I'm not a thief. I'm a wizard doing wizard things. Why don't you run along back to your parents?"

"Wow! A wizard! Cool!" the boy exclaimed, lighting up with excitement.

"Oh great…" Evera thought, rolling her eyes. "Sweetie, I have work to do, and your parents are going to worry about you if you hang out with me too long. Please, just go back to the market."

"Can I see your sword? Ooh, and can you show me some of your magic?"

"No! I told you I have work to do!" Evera snapped, immediately feeling horrible for how she treated the poor child. "Look, I didn't mean to talk like that. I'm just very overwhelmed right now."

The little boy tilted his head, playing with his nose, and then he frolicked off. Evera smiled, watching the boy as he bounced his way back to the market. Her eyes darted around, looking for May, but she was gone. Sighing again, she pursed her lips. Just then, a figure seemingly popped up out of nowhere and asked, "Why are you still here, Evera?"

Looking up, Evera's heart sank and her jaw dropped. "May…" She gasped, stumbling back.

"Sneaking around and watching me, are you? It wasn't enough you stole my sister from me?" May demanded, tears starting to streak her cheeks.

"May, I want to help," Evera began to plead, but the old woman swiftly cut her off.

"Help? You and Lorkai have done nothing but brought me pain!"

"Can't you see that using the ash is poison? Your sister tried to kill us, and it was her own actions that led to her death."

"Stop!" May screamed through sobs. "You wizards are so pious, thinking you can tell people what to do and how to live. The ash never brought the pain that your kind has to Goandria. War and more war, endless fighting for so long that no one even remembers how it all started! The worlox are undefeatable, and fighting them is moot. The best we can do is make the best of a horrible situation and use a bit of their power to get by in this cruel world. But no, you and Lorkai have taken it upon yourselves to be the holy guards of morality and do whatever you can to stop something you can't control. You watching me to find out which seller I purchase the ash from? Well, how about I just tell you?" The old woman thrust her arm toward the vender selling produce. "That is the one. He knows all about you and Lorkai and has been eager to meet you."

"You *were* the one who hired that mercenary!" Evera exclaimed.

"I don't know what you are talking about. I can hardly put food on my table. How could I hire a mercenary?" May asked defensively.

"Isn't it just a little convenient that we part badly and then a mercenary attacks us at the inn?" Evera countered.

"Like I said, I had nothing to do with that, but maybe he knows something about it," May said, motioning to the market again.

Gritting her teeth, Evera stormed off toward the produce merchant. Withdrawing her sword, she pointed it straight out at the man standing behind the counter. "Tell me what's going on here. Now!" the wizard barked.

"What are you talking about? I am a simple merchant. Would you like to buy..."

"Enough with your games. I know you are selling worlox ash!" Evera erupted. All eyes were on her. Murmurs and whispers filtered through the other customers, some of which decided it was a good time to leave the shop.

Without a single hint of fear, the merchant shrugged. "You must be the wizard I have heard about. Your weapons are rather conspicuous. You two have stirred up quite a bit of trouble around here, especially with those old women. Got folks around here scared." Upon hearing those words, the other merchants decided it was time to close shop, and a dozen or so customers hurried off, not wanting to get entangled in the affairs of wizards. Some, however, found themselves driven by curiosity. They inched closer, hoping to get a better view of the drama unfolding.

"Scared? *We* have them scared? *You* are the one they should fear! You sell them substances that have unpredictable side-effects! Yvonne went mad with the stuff and tried to kill us! You are a monster, no better than the worlox," Evera snarled.

"Maybe you see it that way, but I simply offer an alternative for people to better themselves."

"Lies! You only care about profits, not these people's lives. Where are you getting the ash? By the way, I'm shutting you down. Your days as a merchant are over," Evera declared, not caring about the scene she was creating.

At this point, the townspeople who had been silently watching Evera's confrontation with the merchant backed up. Whispers rose between them, and glares and pointing were directed at Evera. "What is she doing? Who does she think she is? What does she think she will accomplish? There's no way she will get out of this alive." Others walked away, shaking their heads in disgust.

All the other did was chuckle. His belly heaved uncontrollably, and his large, red-bearded face flushed like a merry drunk. "I admire your conviction, but you aren't putting an end to anything," he said, slamming a long, narrow hand onto the countertop. The merchant snapped his fingers, and six large, armored men came forward. Each wore different attire: one was encased in bronze scale mail, another in steel-plate armor, two in heavy leather armor, and two in black steel. The men dressed in black armor had a gold leaf insignia etched into their shoulder guards. Evera did not see any sort of defining markings on the others, but she knew what they were as soon as she set eyes upon them. "Mercs," she uttered, grasping her sword tighter.

Chapter 5

Lorkai hit the side of his fist against the cold stone wall. "There has to be a way in," he mumbled. In spite of his best efforts to get through, the iron grate simply was not going to budge from the outside. "I'm so close. I'm so close! Even unguarded, I can't get in," he said under his breath, frustrated, frantically searching for a way into the fortress. He stomped off along the eastern wall, still finding no way to penetrate the sanctum's outer defenses. Lorkai found the same to be true of the northern and western walls. However, where the western and northern walls met, it appeared that something had hit the wall with just enough force to break away a small portion of stone. The chink in the sanctum's armor barely qualified as a hole. It was three feet off the ground and six inches in diameter.

Lorkai's heart sank. "Two steps back," he hissed, beating his fist against the wall again. Out of curiosity, the wizard fingered the broken stone. Beneath a dusting of snow and a thin layer of ice, he saw that the area appeared to be scorched, and some parts of the stone were actually loose. *"Well that's just a little too lucky for me. What's the catch?"* Lorkai thought glumly as he began to peel away the loose chunks little by little. After almost an hour had passed, Lorkai's hands were nearly frostbit, and he had made little progress on the opening. "Indeed, here is the catch I was expecting," he said, shoving his hands inside the sleeves of his cloak. After a few minutes of trying to warm his hands, Lorkai resumed his work. With purple and blue hands and fingers that would hardly move, the wizard eventually managed to pry enough of the broken stone away to squeeze through.

Within, there was only darkness and silence. The sound of water droplets periodically echoed through the vast and empty halls. Sometimes Lorkai stumbled upon a suit of armor strewn on the floor, but otherwise there was no sign of the worlox anywhere. Eventually, Lorkai came across a pile of branches. He tore off a piece of cloth from his tunic, wrapped the end, and ignited it with a bit of flint he carried in his pouch. "There, that's better." He sighed. After some time, the stone hallway widened a bit and led to an iron door. Half expecting it to be locked, Lorkai gently pulled on the handle. To his surprise, the rusty hinges screeched as the door swung completely open. As the wizard stepped from the tunnel, daylight pierced his eyes, which had just gotten used to the darkness. *Lucky that hole was near a maintenance tunnel, otherwise I would have never gotten through.* He had made it past the first of the sanctum's outer defenses, but there was still one more wall to contend with.

The wizard slowly snuck around the wall, hoping to find another fortunate break, but he knew such luck was highly improbable. His steps were soft and deliberate, and he continually looked over his shoulders. Still, no worlox appeared, just more ash and armor lying about. "Did you guys completely destroy yourselves?" he breathed, scanning the ramparts and the wall tops, finding it hard to believe that he had yet to come across any surviving worlox. Lorkai wandered to the back of the second wall and found a small, postern gate that was left wide open with scores of worlox remains lying in front of it. The gate opened to an archway carved through the wall only large enough for one man to comfortably pass through. The relatively tiny size of the passage made Lorkai question the point of it, since many worlox would be too large to fit. After several paces, Lorkai came to a crossroad in the passageway. To the left a set of stone stairs spiraled upward, and to the right another set of stairs descended underground.

Thankful that he had thought ahead and made a torch, Lorkai headed for the right stairway. Every so often, the pitter-patter of tiny feet darted along the floor, accompanied by a series of squeaks. "Rats." Lorkai shuddered. The stairs took him downward for what Lorkai guessed to be one hundred or more steps, eventually arriving at yet another dark, windowless hallway. The stone corridor stretched on for another hundred feet or more, where there was another choice to take a stairway either up or down.

Stone, stone, and look, more stone. These sanctums all look the same. No detail and no art, except for a few minor enhancements outside. Lorkai thought, traveling down another long flight of stairs. *This must lead to the catacombs and dungeons below the sanctum. If only I could remember for sure.* After he had finished the set of stairs, he took a seat on the bottom step, hunching over his knees slightly. Panting, Lorkai rubbed his knees gently, and after a couple minutes, he stood back up and made his way down yet another dark, stone tunnel. Off in the distance somewhere, Lorkai thought he caught the faint sound of metal clanking and something hissing, yet nothing was visible. "More darkness and more stone." Lorkai sighed, pressing onward. After some time had passed, Lorkai noticed there was a faint glimmer of red-orange light streaming into the far end of the hall. Lorkai half-trotted down the corridor, excited to see some sort of light. The closer he came to the light, the louder the din became. When he reached the end of the corridor he had hoped to see sunlight or torchlight, but instead he found dozens of furnaces. Streams of molten metal flowed through the room in square-like patterns from one furnace to another. Bellows pumped air that the fires greedily devoured, and hammers rang without ceasing.

"No one around, yet they keep working? This day just keeps getting stranger," the wizard mumbled to himself.

The workers were diminutive beings with pale, off-white skin. Their flesh was blotchy with open sores, most of which were found around the eyes and mouths of the creatures. Lorkai guessed they were close to a foot tall, and most had brilliant, bright blue eyes that nearly glowed. Despite how small they were, the little creatures managed to carry several weapons at a time and use hammers larger than their heads. *These creatures don't look like worlox. I, at least, never heard of worlox such as these. Perhaps they are some worker drone race the others enslave? Though since when do worlox have eyes that blue? These poor things look miserable.* He wrestled internally with whether or not he should approach them and ask for direction, but Lorkai also did not know how loyal they were to their masters. For all the wizard knew, the creatures could betray him. The other issue, though, was that he could be wandering around for hours or days, or he may never find his way and die in the dank pits of the sanctum. Lorkai realized more than ever that the outer structure of the sanctum was just for show. The network of underground passages could possibly be endless. It seemed to him that the real sanctum was beneath the surface.

Lorkai decided that ultimately his best choice was to risk talking to the slaves and see if they could offer any sense of direction so he was not wandering around forever. He cautiously stepped forward, unsure of the best way to approach them. *Are they friendly? Will they fear me?* His heartbeat quickened as he inched forward. At first, no one appeared to notice the newcomer in the forge area. The small beings scurried around frantically, hardly paying any mind to their kin, let alone their surroundings. Lorkai approached one who was madly striking his hammer against what looked like an incomplete breastplate. "Excuse me," he said softly, hoping not to startle it. When nothing happened, Lorkai repeated himself. This time, the creature jumped and looked wide-eyed at the wizard, shrieked, and scurried back into a small, hut-like structure.

"Wait! I'm not here to hurt you. I…ugh, never mind," Lorkai said, throwing his hands up into the air. *Maybe someone else will be more reasonable,* the wizard thought as he noticed hundreds of little eyes staring at him. All work had come to an abrupt halt, and an uncomfortable silence now hung in the air.

"Uhh, hello?" Lorkai said awkwardly, unsure of what to do next. At the sound of his voice, many of the little beings scattered, but some stayed out of curiosity. Lorkai stood straighter. Eyeing the creatures back, he said,

"Hello, my name is Lorkai. I am a wizard. I'm not here to hurt you. I need your help." ~~Then he thought to himself,~~ *~~"It looks like they need my help more than I need theirs, though."~~* A few crept forward, studying Lorkai as if they had never seen a man before. Some briefly touched his side or his leg and then hastily backed away.

"A wizard?" one asked. He was slightly taller than some of his kin.

"Yes, I'm a wizard. I would like someone to direct me to the dungeons. I have friends there I need to save, and once I find them, I will free you as well."

They all looked at one another and mumbled whisperings Lorkai could not quite understand. "A wizard?" he asked again. "That is impossible." His little hand waved.

Lorkai's brow furrowed. "Why?"

"The masters said you were all dead, that everyone was dead. Humans, englifs, the rest of the ferrorians…"

"No, the worlox tried to do that, but so far they haven't. How long have you been down here?"

"We don't know. It's been long. So very long. We never see the world outside, and only rarely see the masters. Until recently, that is, when they wanted to build up their armory again."

"So you don't know that your masters are dead? Well, most likely dead. There is no one around. The worlox have some sort of civil war going on, and it looks like the armies that fought here eradicated themselves."

"You are a liar, some trickster. Be gone." Theferrorian waved him off.

"I'm not a liar! Look for yourselves!"

"We know about the battle, but the masters are not all dead. You are trying to trick us."

"I am not," Lorkai said defensively. "I came in here and did not see a single worlox. How do you think I got this far?"

"That proves nothing. Now be gone, I said! We don't like liars."

"Why are you so convinced I am trying to deceive you?"

"The masters do many things to trick us, and the masters cannot be killed. Besides, just before you showed up, I saw one of them going to the dungeons." The ferrorian's eyes narrowed as they focused on the wizard more intently. "That is where you are going."

"Yes. Like I said, I have come to save my friends, and I will get you out, too."

"That's if you aren't a liar."

"What can I do to prove I am who I say I am?" Lorkai asked, immediately dreading what the creature would suggest, but he needed to find the other wizards, especially if another worlox was going to interrogate them, or worse.

The ferrorian thought a moment, then his eyes widened abruptly. "Hand me your sword."

"My sword? It's bigger than you are!" Lorkai blurted.

"My kinsmen will keep it safe. Don't you worry."

"How do I know I can trust *you*? The same standard applies to you too."

"You are far more dangerous than I am. If I guide you to someplace unsavory or you feel betrayed, it will be far easier for you to keep me to my word than it is for me to keep you to yours."

"Fine, just be sure not to lose it," Lorkai said, reluctantly handing the weapon to a group of ferrorians. "Now, take me to the dungeons."

"As you wish, master wizard."

The ferrorian led Lorkai down even more dark, stone corridors. Over and over they traversed a dark hall, turned and went down some steps, and repeated the process until Lorkai felt as if he had walked ten miles underground. For such a small creature, the ferrorian moved rather quickly. Lorkai felt somewhat winded trying to keep up. Lorkai lost track of time, but he guessed it was an hour or two later when the dungeons were at last in sight. Two torches hung on the wall on either side of rounded, double, iron doors.

"Odd, there is no light anywhere in this sanctum except for those two torches," Lorkai remarked.

The small creature remained quiet, but his eyes flared a bit, and he stepped back slowly upon seeing the doorway. "One of the masters is here," he breathed harshly.

Lorkai tipped his torch forward to get a better look at the doorway, and he saw that the left door stood out from the other about a half-inch. "That's not good, and I don't have my sword."

"This is where we must part, wizard," the ferrorian said, backing up more, watching the doors as if they were about to come alive at any moment.

"Hey, wait a minute. We had a deal. Until I get my sword back, you are stuck with me."

"But, in *there*? With one of *them*?" the creature shuddered.

"Yes, now come on."

Sheepishly, the ferrorian bowed his head, reluctantly obeying. With a groan, the slave pushed the door open, allowing enough room for him and Lorkai to slide through. Inside, there was a massive circular chamber with torches lining the wall. Six hallways branched out from the central room, also lit with the dancing, orange-yellow glow of torchlight. Blood-curdling screams periodically filled the halls, sending chills along the wizard's spine. It was much warmer in the detention area, but the warmth offered no comfort. It felt oppressive and taunting, like all the pain and suffering seeped out into the air.

"I believe the ones you are looking for are this way. The masters have taken a lot of interest in them." The ferrorian led Lorkai toward the northeastern hallway.

A few paces down, an awful stench stung the wizard's nostrils. Coughing a couple times, he covered his face with his right hand and looked around for the origin of the foul smell. He noticed rows upon rows of rusted iron cages as far as he could see on either side. Just above the cells were rows of torches, and between them, he saw spears bolted to the wall with severed heads sheathing their tips.

"I thought I smelled rotting flesh." Lorkai gagged.

"The masters' trophies of victory. Some are from battles, but most are prisoners who no longer proved to be useful. You had better pray none of your friends ended up like that."

"How much farther? I do not know if I can take any more of this horrid smell. The sooner we get out of here, the better for all of us."

"It's a little way yet, but not too far."

"Ugh, I can hardly breathe. Doesn't the smell bother you?" Lorkai asked as another scream echoed in their ears.

Mice, rats, spiders, and even scorpions pattered the along cell area. Some spiders made their homes on the gruesome trophies near the torches, while the rats and mice were content with occasionally scurrying at the edges of Lorkai's peripheral vision. All of the cells were afflicted by the cancer of rust, causing the floor to be stained red. Lorkai wondered how much longer they would even be able to hold prisoners before completely rotting away.

"Hey, hey, stop! There is someone inside this one," Lorkai called out to his guide. The ferrorian casually turned around to eye the wizard before quickly looking at the ground again.

"Is he alive?" the creature asked, peeking around behind the wizard.

"I can't tell."

"Then leave him. If he isn't dead yet, he soon will be, whether you get him out or not."

Half of Lorkai's face scrunched up. "How could you say something so horrible?"

"We don't have time. If a master is here, we need to free the ones you came for and go." The ferrorian hissed and continued walking. Lorkai gritted his teeth, looking at the captive.

"No, I will save him. All who oppose the worlox will soon find sanctuary, and I will not abandon anyone," he stated confidently, placing his hands on the iron bars. Lorkai's left palm glowed as the lock melted away. Swinging the door open hastily, Lorkai leapt inside. Cradling the stranger's head, he felt for a pulse, and with a flash of his eyes, he called out over his shoulder, "He is still alive!"

"I told you he won't be for long. He won't be able to make it out of here. Now leave him! A master is near. We must not dawdle."

Lorkai shook his head, gazing upon the poor, emaciated soul. He gently placed the man back down. "I will come back for you," Lorkai whispered, rushing to catch up with his guide.

"I thought you wizards had to use your special swords to perform any magic," the ferrorian said with heavy suspicion.

"For the most part, but we have limited use without it. That is why you wanted my sword to be left in the forge, isn't it?"

"Here we are. We are getting close," said the ferrorian. "They should be in one of these. This is where the masters have come the most."

"Wait, if you are working in the forges, how do you know where the worlox even go? I mean you didn't even know they were all dead."

"I do more than forge work, master wizard."

Ignoring the diminutive being, Lorkai ran ahead. There, at last, he saw the captives he had spent so long searching for. There were two or three per cell, all seventeen alive but gaunt, pale, and hunched over.

"Emir! Wulaf!" Lorkai cried as he came to the first cell that contained his friends. "It's me, Lorkai! I've come to get you out of here."

Chapter 6

"Lorkai! You came! You actually came back for us!" A woman named Closna exclaimed, falling to her knees in tears.

"I told you I would. We have to finish the work we started if we are to end this war so it does not continue in another generation."

"How did you get in here?" another wizard asked with a voice so deep it seemed to vibrate the stone and metal.

"There seems to be a civil war amongst the worlox, and as far as I can tell, they completely destroyed themselves. There may be a few stragglers lurking around, though."

Lorkai quickly worked to melt away the locks on the cells, and once all the wizards were freed, he turned to the ferrorian and said, "Now take me back to the forges." Before the creature could respond, a *clank, tink* reverberated in the distance.

The diminutive being simply shrieked and cowered behind Lorkai upon seeing a fiery glow abruptly engulf the far end of the dungeon.

"What is it?" the wizard asked.

"A mas-ster," the creature trembled.

"Come, we need to move! Now!" Lorkai shouted. "Is there any other way out of here?" His guide simply stood with his feet rooted to the floor, his eyes locked on the light that was growing brighter. Lorkai gently shook the ferrorian. "Do you want your freedom? Do you want to never have to serve the worlox again? You need to snap out of it! You need to help us, or we will all be dead. That glow means a worlox is coming, and without our weapons, we are no match for it."

"Yes." He shook his head. "Yes, turn around. There is a small passage at the back of the dungeon used mainly for us ferrorians, but it might be difficult for people of your size to navigate."

"Considering our circumstances, I think it's worth trying," Lorkai replied.

All eighteen wizards squeezed behind their guide into a cave-like formation that the sanctum seemed to be built around. At the far back of the cell wing, there was a tiny crevice, barely noticeable in the dim light, marking the entry to the cavern. Each wizard had to crawl on all fours, making travel excruciatingly slow. Sometimes the path would grow even narrower, forcing some to improvise by twisting and turning so they wouldn't get permanently stuck. Lorkai could not safely take his torch with, and the only light provided in the miniature cave system was the ferrorian's, which was relative to his size and offered minimal illumination.

"Gah! Maybe it's a good thing those blasted worlox didn't feed us much," a male wizard grumbled near the back.

"Speaking of, do you guys think you can make it out of here?" Lorkai asked, but he realized his question sounded more like an afterthought than genuine concern for their well-being. "Do any of you need a rest? It is a long way out."

"We just want to get out of here," someone said, accompanied by several nods.

Okay, stupid question, but I wonder how they will all get out of here alive without their full strength.

For almost a full hour, the wizards wound their way through the cavern. Lorkai was the first to emerge behind the ferrorian. Standing fully erect, he placed his hands on his lower back for a minute or two and then continued to stretch his arms and neck. "It's nice to be out of such a dank, dark hole," he commented, brushing off his soggy pants.

"It looks like the englif wizards may have fared a bit better," the ferrorian said with a slight smile. Then with narrow eyes and a contemptuous tone, he eyed the four englifs, who were a bit taller than their human comrades. Two had fair skin, and the other two were slightly darker. All four of them had green eyes, but one had flecks of light blue in his iris that twinkled each time he turned his head, somewhat resembling starlight. The other three were females with varying degrees of a blue-green mixture in their eyes, but green was the overall dominant color. Aside from their eyes, the most striking difference between the englifs and their human cohorts were their brilliant, white teeth, even in spite of the harsh conditions of the dungeons. "Shape shifters and traitors," the ferrorian suddenly spat. "Your kind have such power, yet for the most part, they retreated to your island sanctuary of Caldaria, the one place in Goandria the masters have not reached yet."

The male englif, whose name was Drystom, stepped forward. His eyes shone brightly in the light of the ferrorian's torch as he puffed his chest and hardened his expression. "Not all englifs are the same, and your criticisms of my kind can apply to yours as well, runt."

"Hey, come on. We can't do this now," Lorkai pleaded.

"He's right. Just let it go, Drystom," one of the englif women chimed in.

"Yes. We need to know where exactly we are because none of this looks familiar," said Lorkai.

"We looped around the dungeons to the corridor adjacent to the forges. You must trust me, master wizard. I know where I'm going."

"This was a lot faster way to and from the dungeons," Lorkai commented.

"Yes, but would you really want to squeeze through there twice?" asked the ferrorian.

"No, probably not."

"We still have several paces to go before we reach the forges anyway, master wizard." Just then, a screech rumbled from within the dungeons, followed by three tremors that shook and cracked the floor and nearby walls. "A mas-ster! We mus-st hurry!" the ferrorian cried, racing onward as fast as his little legs could carry him.

"Hey! Wait," Lorkai yelled out, but soon the wizards' guide was out of sight.

"Who knew someone so small could run so fast," Drystom said.

"Now what are we going to do? We can't run after the little creature," another wizard said warily.

"Well, for the time being, we will do what we can and go the same direction he went and hope we end up in the same place. After all, there is apparently a worlox warlord looking for you, and it has realized you escaped, and I am going to need to get my sword back."

"Why did you have to trust that cowardly little creature to help you?" Drystom asked.

"What was I supposed to do, wander for days or weeks in this labyrinth until I found you? Remember, Drystom, I was the one who saved you when I didn't have to, and I am still your general. Be careful how you speak to me."

"Forgive me, general."

"Lorkai, how do you propose we follow the ferrorian? He took with him the only light we had."

"There is still a bit of light at the far end of the hall, and we can feel our way along the walls, Hewlan. Your shape-shifting abilities may also come in handy," said Lorkai.

"We are too weak for that," replied the englif.

"I figured as much but hoped otherwise. We will get out of here, I promise. We haven't made it this far just to fail," Lorkai said, clasping Hewlan on the shoulder.

Twenty more minutes passed as the wizards stumbled along in the darkness before a dim light appeared at the northern end of the passage, signaling a corner they had not seen. "Come on, wizards, you are almost there!" a familiar voice said.

"The ferrorian coward!" snarled Drystom.

"Calm down. This is a good thing. At least we know where we are now. See, the forges are right over there." Lorkai pointed.

Back in the forges, things looked exactly as they were when Lorkai had left. Scores of ferrorians dashed about like mice, hammering away on the anvils, hauling weapons, or working the bellows. Lorkai ignored the bewildered stares and jabbering amongst the slaves and walked straight up to the one who had been his guide. "I think it's time I got my sword back."

"Yes, yes, of course, master wizard." The ferrorian motioned to three others who swiftly ducked inside a tent and brought the weapon back to its owner.

"Now to get out of here," he breathed. Then, raising his voice, he turned to the ferrorian people. "I promised you I would free you once my people were saved. You have kept up your agreement, and now I will fulfill mine. Put down your tools. You are no longer slaves to the demons! You are free to go where you will, to find other ferrorian settlements, or to do whatever it is you are called to do."

With the aid of their guide once again, Lorkai, the wizards, and the remaining ferrorians made the hour-and-a-half trek back to the surface of the sanctum. Lorkai was surprised that it did not take longer, despite the many breaks they took for the sake of the wizards. *How they manage to keep moving is something I can't understand. By the looks of them, they should just collapse right where they are and never get up.*

"The sun at last!" Emir exclaimed, shielding his face.

"Yes, but it hurts," a wizard added.

"And evening will soon be upon us," Lorkai added.

"Where do we go from here?" Closna asked.

"That's the problem," Lorkai said with a deep exhale. "There is no food, and the nearest village is miles away."

"There is the geyser. Its power would be more than enough to sustain us. It would do far more than any food," suggested Drystom.

"We still have not gotten out of the sanctum yet, either. It looks like we are in some sort of courtyard, but it's hard to say for sure. Worlox architecture is so strange." Closna wiped her matted, red hair out of her eyes.

"More stone. You would think that a courtyard would maybe have something other than stonework. Stone floor, stone walls, and look, stone statues!" Lorkai remarked.

"Yes, this is where the masters honor their heroes," the ferrorian guide said.

"What is that at the foot of the statues?" Emir asked.

"I wouldn't be bothered by that if I were you. It is best not to poke around too much in the home of the mas… I mean worlox," the little creature warned, but the wizard was far too curious and paid him no mind.

Emir's tall and spindly frame tramped over to one of the ten statues and knelt down, brushing away some of the snow. His bushy eyebrows narrowed and his head cocked. He suddenly shrieked and recoiled. "They're bones! Piles of bones arranged in some sort of pattern!"

Lorkai shook his head. "You were warned, weren't you? This is a worlox sanctum. What did you expect to find? We still need to get out of the sanctum, and as I have said already, night will soon be here."

"Oh, you will not have to worry about that, little wizards," a deep, vaguely-female voice echoed in the background. "Oh, you ants thought you could run from me. How cute."

"The master! The master!" The ferrorians squealed, withdrawing to the doorway from which they had just emerged.

"The worlox are not your masters anymore," Lorkai said to the creatures. Drawing his weapon from its scabbard, he addressed the female voice. "Why don't you come out of the shadows? Why hide from a bunch of former-slaves and emaciated wizards?"

To the right of the group stood a dark-gray wall that was about eight or nine feet high and nine yards long. The wall seemed strangely out of place, for it did not support any other structure, and it did not connect to the outer two defensive walls or even the citadel. The wall was simply there. A few seconds after Lorkai's words were spoken, the center of this wall exploded into hundreds of splinters of pebbles and rocks. Some of the larger pieces hit some nearby ferrorians, killing or severely injuring them. Through the impromptu hole in the wall stepped two large, lizard-like feet tipped with claws.

"Do you dare suggest I am a coward?" the worlox hissed between her fangs.

"You! I've seen you before, leading the charge against another worlox army. You must be responsible for the fact that none of your kind still live here. I suppose a thank you is in order since you made my job much easier than I originally anticipated. Still, I'm surprised to see you alive, which must mean you are either slow or incompetent."

"If the worlox who challenge me are mere insects squished beneath my feet, what do you suppose you are, oh wizard? I have heard of you, Lorkai. You're the general and also one of the few who discovered something very precious. In fact, all the wizards here have, which means I only need one to live if you refuse to help me, which of course I assume will be the case."

"What is your goal? To destroy your own kind, and destroy Goandria itself? In the hundreds of years this war has been going on, I have never read about a worlox starting an uprising from within. Have you gotten bored?" Lorkai quipped.

"You think you can hide behind sarcasm? You should bow to me; I am the new goddess of Goandria, the queen of darkness. If you were wise, you would bow before me instead of obstinately opposing me. What chance do you think you have?"

"You are a queen of nothing, Zeneth, and a goddess only in your own eyes. We still collectively rule the worlox. You have gained a victory, but with that victory you lost your armies," a male voice declared from within the sanctum.

"Vox!" Zeneth exclaimed, craning her neck upward.

"I must say, your plan nearly worked…nearly. As always, your arrogance blinds you. If you would have actually destroyed us all, your victory would have been doubtless, but alas, the Citheara remain! You should have made sure we were all dead before you sought out the wizards. Poor Zeneth, if only you knew what fate awaits you. From within these chambers, we are safe."

"Ahhh!" Zeneth screamed, tossing a sphere of black magic at the balcony where Vox and two other worlox warlords stood. The ebony ball dissipated as it hit an invisible barrier in front of them.

Dozens of horns sounded from the eastern, western, and southern regions near the sanctum. "You are trapped, traitor," one of the warlords said with a wide grin on his face, revealing his half-rotten teeth.

"No! No!" Zeneth screeched, slamming her fists into the remaining portion of the wall.

Lorkai whispered over his shoulder to Drystom, "We have to leave now, while the worlox are distracted. There is an army coming, and if we get caught in the middle, we will never get out."

The other wizards silently nodded in agreement. Lorkai knelt down and murmured to his ferrorian friend, "It's time to leave. We can sneak out while they are distracted. It looks like the Citheara are more concerned with Zeneth than us."

"The masters still live. We will be caught!" the creature protested.

"We will get caught if we just stay here! Didn't you hear that? Worlox armies are coming. We don't want to be here for that."

Whether the ferrorian heard him or not, Lorkai could not say, for the creature just stood open-mouthed, gazing up at his former slave-masters.

"The runts have become a liability," Drystom whispered in Lorkai's ear.

"You're right," Lorkai acknowledged slowly. "We leave them and head for the geyser. It should be less than a half day's walk from here. Let's go."

"What about them?" an englif asked, inclining her head toward the ferrorians.

"We are going without them." Lorkai shook his head.

"But…" another wizard began.

"Those are my orders. My first priority is what is best for you. I can find the way out from here."

While the wizards crept silently away, the worlox armies moved in. Thousands of infantry completely surrounded the sanctum and sifted their way into the fortress. Zeneth quickly searched for an exit, but she found none. She got down on her knees before the Citheara. "Fools! Do you not know what knowledge those wizards hold? We should join forces and find that fissure."

"The wizards are of no consequence, but you, Zeneth, are a risk we cannot afford to keep," Vox answered.

"Soon we will find the fissure on our own, without the wizards. Let them flee. They will die soon anyway. We are worlox after all, lords of Goandria, and nothing is beyond our grasp," another warlord professed from behind the other three.

Chapter 7

Six swords moved in, their points glinting in the sunlight, waiting to strike at the lone wizard. "You're outmatched, wizard," the merchant gloated. "Why don't you run along now?"

Evera said nothing and stood her ground. In a flash, the weapons were upon her like a metal whirlwind. After parrying a few blows, Evera managed to knock two mercenaries back and disarm another. Still, the other three continued their assault. Strike after strike, they pounded their swords into Evera's, yet the nimble woman managed to block every time. She clenched her jaw and looked each mercenary in the eyes, daring them to make their next move while her own blade became rimmed with a blazing, green glow. One of the mercenaries in black armor heavily stomped a foot forward and heaved his two-handed weapon over his head, bringing it down against Evera's sword. The wizard stumbled back. Seeing an opportunity to gain the upper hand, he swiped his sword to the left, but the merc's attack did not have the desired outcome. Evera stepped aside with lightning speed, and her blade hit the mercenary's gauntlets, causing the large weapon to clank to the ground. Before he could retrieve his weapon, Evera slammed her pommel into his face.

With their strength reduced in a matter of minutes, the mercenaries turned and ran. "Where are you going? I paid you to do a job! She is just one wizard!" the merchant shouted, beating his fist repeatedly against the countertop.

"It looks like you lost your leverage," said Evera. "Now show me where you stash it."

"Look, this is just a big misunderstanding."

"Show me!"

"Okay, okay, it's back here."

Evera followed him a short way into the back of the small shop. Piled in the back right corner were six crates, each filled with vials of worlox ash. "Here it is," the man said reluctantly. Evera knelt down, touched the tip of her sword to the bottom crate, and whispered what seemed to the merchant a long string of babbling. With a *swoosh*, the crates were engulfed in yellow-green fire.

"We done now?" the man asked, folding his arms across his chest.

"Oh, not even close. You broke the law, and you sold an illegal substance that affected many lives. My friend was one of them. You are coming with me back to the temple. There you are going to tell the magister and the council everything you know so we can get a handle on this situation."

"You can't do this to me!"

"Can't I?"

"Then you need to arrest everyone who has ever bought from me. Some probably resold it themselves," he protested.

"But you are at the core of this issue. I am a wizard, and it is my responsibility to hold the people accountable. Now turn around," Evera ordered. He obeyed, and she tied his hands with a bit of rope she had on her. "What's your name?" she then asked.

"Rolaph. Now please untie me. I'm not an animal."

"Where is that arrogant bravado you demonstrated just a few minutes ago? Did you realize you bit off more than you could chew? You should know that trying to trap a wizard is very unwise." Evera closed her eyes and exhaled, and after a few deep breaths, her eyelids reopened. "Everything just got way out of hand, but I decided to help the people here the best I can, and if the only thing I can do is turn you in, then so be it."

"I…I'm sorry, miss!" Rolaph squealed pathetically.

"You are sorry? You were just gloating when you thought I wasn't going to win. Now you think I will believe you? One thing is for sure: I am not walking the whole way back to the temples. We are going to find a horse and a wagon, and you are going to sit in the wagon and keep quiet. Do you understand?"

"Aw, please! Please! You are a decent lady, you have to be to be a wizard. Show me some mercy!" Rolaph continued to beg. He even got down on his knees and cried like a toddler.

"This is the merciful thing for me to do. For Grivear, that is. On second thought, why don't *you* buy the horse and wagon? I'm sure someone around here sells them."

"You're cold, ma'am, just cold."

"I am when the ones I love are put in danger and I see an addiction eat away at a couple of old women. Look, I actually do get it. I understand that the wizards have not been fulfilling their promises as they should. I get that the war has eaten away at so much decency in the world, even within our own ranks. I really do understand why you have done this. You are desperate, like so many here. If you buy the horse and wagon, I will do everything

I can to make sure the magister shows mercy on you. I will say you went willingly, and I will leave out the part about the mercs you hired to trap me."

"Fine. I can agree to that, ma'am," Rolaph said, slumping his head.

Two hours later, the horse and wagon were purchased. Evera rode on the horse, and Rolaph sat in the small cart behind it. The brown steed with white spots whinnied as it clomped along. At first, it seemed content to merely trot, in spite of Evera's urging to the contrary. It looked around and strutted like it somehow found a new appreciation for life, not caring one bit about the goading of its new mistress or the load behind. Once they were about five miles from the village, the steed took off at a full gallop.

Evera breathed an exasperated sigh and soon became lost in her own thoughts amidst the snowy backdrop. In her mind, she saw the temples and felt the scorn of her leaving without the permission of her superiors. *It is going to be hard facing the magister, or anyone there, after what Lorkai and I did. Will I be expelled or suspended or something else? I wanted so badly to get away from my scrolls and do something important. Maybe this is my chance. This adventure turned out nothing like I expected. I will be more than content to return to my scrolls after all this is over and record my journey and experiences. Knowing the council, though, they will have more than enough history for me to transcribe. That is, if I am ever allowed to do that again. The magister is not known to be a gentle man. He sees things in only black or white, good or bad, and of course, his will represents good. It stands to reason that Lorkai and I will face some kind of disciplinary action. I wonder if the magisters of the other temples are like that, too.*

"Hey!" Rolaph shouted out. "What is going to happen to me?"

"It would probably be best for you to just be quiet right now and not dwell on it," Evera said.

"That bad, huh?" the merchant pushed.

Evera shrugged and tried to remain stoic. "I really don't know what your fate will be. We haven't had to deal with a situation like this in a long time, if ever. I guess there had to be a reason for the wizards outlawing use of the ash, but I suppose most of them guessed no one would be stupid enough to actually try it."

"It's a living, and I haven't seen any proof that it's *that* bad," Rolaph said.

"I thought you were sorry. Since you had some sort of deal with May, I am guessing you know what happened to Yvonne."

"You killed her. She told me all about it."

"I didn't kill her. Did May conveniently leave out the part where Yvonne was so steeped in the power of the ash that she turned violent and used an unnatural sorcery to try to kill us first?"

"Is that supposed to make it right?" Rolaph rolled his eyes.

"Watch it. Don't forget it is your fault this situation occurred to begin with. What happened to the pathetic fool who groveled at my feet?"

Again he shrugged. "It was not an act I could keep up."

Evera's knuckles turned white with the horse's reins in their grip. She entertained the idea of drawing in the reins, climbing down from the horse, and putting a fear into Rolaph he had never known before. *That is something Lorkai would do,* she thought. A grin reflexively formed on her face. She couldn't help but think of her friend and how he would quickly whip this man's attitude into shape. The wizard resolved to not feed the fire Rolaph was attempting to set, so she said no more to him.

She thought she heard Rolaph mumble more insults under his breath, or perhaps she was reading into it. No matter what was or wasn't said, Evera kept a smile on her face and shifted her focus to the setting sun. *There is a terrible war, demons everywhere, yet there is so much wonder and beauty in Goandria. Oh, how easy it is to forget, though. What was it like for our ancestors before the worlox came? Sure, I read about it, chronicled much of the known histories from then, but that cannot possibly capture the entire essence of the time. I believe we can return to better times again. There seems to be a shift in the atmosphere. Something tells me the reign of the worlox will end soon.*

Even after the sun sank below the horizon, Evera still spurred the steed on, and they continued through the night. A couple hours after sunset, Rolaph fell asleep in spite of the jarring and creaking of the wagon. The simple, two-wheeled wagon was made of heavy wood, but much of it was gray and rotten. Clearly the last owners had failed to take care of it, and Evera kept expecting it to fly apart at the next hole or dip they came across. "How he can sleep through all this is astounding," the wizard uttered to herself.

Well into the night the horse galloped. The stars above glinted like diamonds stuck in a black tapestry, and no cloud dared to shroud the moon's half-light on that crisp, winter evening. Even with weariness growing more prominent, Evera refused to give in. Gripping the reins tightly, she clenched her jaw, focusing on the task at hand. After hours of travel, the wooded path leading to the blessed temples was finally in sight. She eased up on the reins, allowing the horse to slow to a trot while it traversed the familiar gravel road shrouded with a thick row of forestry on both sides.

Before her, the blazing white towers rose up. "Home at last." Evera breathed deeply with both joy and apprehension.

Chapter 8

Amidst the snow and ice was a rocky region with a few scattered trees. It looked like the rocks were placed intentionally by something or someone as a marker, but the eyes that saw it did not care in the moment. Their concern was what flowed from a large crevice in the limestone. The dark green substance shimmered as it flowed from the ground, bending the light around it like a prism. It appeared to be some mystical water that streamed up, but it wasn't water. As its guests came closer, it began to pulsate with veins of red throughout the green body, and the geyser began to gush even higher and more forcefully.

The wizards rushed to the geyser with all of their remaining strength. Some limped, some ran, but all hurried as if heading to a feast when they had not eaten in weeks. When Lorkai came closer, something burned within him, but it was not passion or longing for what the energy had to offer. Lorkai looked at the back of his hands and saw streaks of black appearing under his skin. At first it was just a nuisance to him, but when he was merely yards away from the streaming energy, his chest burned like a fire had erupted within, and he collapsed to his knees, his eyes watering from the pain.

"I told you, didn't I? I told you this was your destiny," a voice whispered. "I am becoming stronger with every decision you make."

"You…" Lorkai coughed.

"I am the real you. I am the one who will give you strength, who led you here. This is where I was born, but as I said, your decisions helped me grow."

The wizard groaned. His mind raced, and confusion set in. He longed for comfort, longed for nourishment, and there it was! Just a short distance from him, the geyser flowed, and it could imbue him with a strength far better than any meal. Lorkai crawled forward, reaching out his right hand into the very center of the energy that spilled from the ground. The pain and confusion receded, and his mind felt clear. Strength flowed through his muscles, and a power ignited within him.

Standing fully erect, he saw that all eyes were upon him. Looking at his hands, he saw the black, veiny streaks had become more pronounced. His eyes moved to a large tree, and with a snap of his fingers, it splintered into mere woodchips and leaves. The other wizards stumbled back, their wide eyes still set on their general. A few others tried to do the same to other trees, but only managed to make them sway.

"This is the new era of the wizard order, my friends," Lorkai began, making eye contact with each of them individually as he spoke. "With this power, we can conquer the worlox! We can lead our order to victory. No longer are we bound by the old ways and rules that restricted our magic. This, my friends, is the answer we have been searching for. If all the wizards would dip their hands into this energy, we would become more powerful than all the worlox in Goandria."

The other wizards applauded, cheering and chanting his name. Drystom then approached the general. "With these new powers, we will become invincible. It seems that each time we recharged with this new magic, we become stronger, but for some reason it affects you differently. Your power is far more potent than ours."

"I noticed that too, and the pain I felt. None of you seemed to experience it, though," Lorkai said.

"Pain? No, I did not feel any pain when we got here."

"And I suppose that means you don't have this, either?" Lorkai asked, twisting his arm outward to show the other wizard the black, veiny streaks on the back of his hand.

"No." Drystom shook his head. "What do you think it is from?"

Lorkai chewed his lower lip as he ~~thought~~ pondered on it. "I was poisoned by a worlox blade, and some old crones used a remedy with worlox ash to heal me. This is probably one of the side effects." Then Lorkai recalled the voice he had heard, and fear mixed with excitement washed over him. "The specter wolf," he whispered.

"What?" Drystom asked.

"Have you ever received strange visions?" Lorkai asked.

"Strange visions?"

"Yes ~~Yeah~~..." Lorkai trailed off, hoping he would not have to go into any more detail.

"I'm not sure what you mean."

"It didn't start right away, but just before I left the temples to free you, I had these dreams of a being telling me that I am to become a powerful ruler of Goandria. At first, I thought it was just a nightmare, but it eventually felt more and more real."

Drystom smirked and shook his head. "I think you were right the first time. It was just a bad dream."

"Wait, I have experienced something similar. Was yours of a black hooded figure with glowing blue eyes?" Another englif joined in.

Chills ran down Lorkai's spine. "Something like that, Xiom, yes."

"I blew it off at first too, but it became more persistent. The robed figure would say that it was my future, that I would become a conqueror of Goandria and have unrivaled power. It first occurred a little while after we first utilized the power here. Do you think there is a connection?"

"Maybe. Mine said this is where he was born. Every time it appeared to me, I felt darkness and an aura of dread."

Xiom nodded. "Me too. A side effect of the new magic, maybe? Is this a sign, a warning?" she asked.

"This is the edge we need over the worlox. We cannot give that up." Lorkai's eyes flared, and his voice slightly trembled as he spoke. "This war has gone on long enough. We must do everything we can to bring it to an end. No matter the cost, no matter the sacrifice!" Lorkai's heartrate increased and his brow wrinkled. "I did not exactly mean to say it like that. Sometimes words just come out of my mouth, and it feels like I have no control."

"Things you don't mean to say?" Drystom asked, sounding more intrigued than concerned.

"I don't know. I can't explain it. I feel different. Neither good nor bad, just different. Like there is another will inside me beyond my own. I do understand your concerns, though. What these visions mean, I don't really know. I'm not even sure it should matter anymore. What if what we thought was right was actually wrong? The wizards have drilled into us and our ancestors a definition of what is and is not the right way to use magic. Have these ways produced an effective method to use against our enemies? No, it merely keeps them at bay."

"Should we stop using this? We don't even know for sure where this stream of energy comes from," Xiom said.

"It is very probable it comes from the worlox's realm."

"Lorkai is right," interjected Drystom. "What have the old ways done but cause more death and destruction? Can we really argue that what we were taught to be right is really good?"

"This line of thought could be very dangerous, but I agree, Lorkai. If we surrender this power when we know it could help, then we have failed Goandria."

"But we cannot stop using it!" Lorkai faced Xiom.

"We now have an edge in this war. Soon, we will have the power to obliterate large swaths of our enemy," said another wizard.

"I did say at whatever cost, too. That must be our focus, to end this war no matter what it does to us. We cannot allow further generations to experience this oppression. This geyser could kill us. That is the simple truth of the matter. Wizards were not intended to wield power such as this. I'm sure you all could feel it. Our natural *talents* are diminishing in this area. I struggled to do a simple healing spell on myself. Voshnore is abandoning us."

"Isn't that a sign we should stop?" Closna added. "It is he who endowed us with these powers to begin with. It is all so confusing."

"We have found another way, though. I have fought with this internally as well. You are right in saying Voshnore is the source of our powers. However, how long will we have to fight in a never-ending battle with those demons? How long until Goandria is safe? He has heard the prayers of the people for hundreds of years, and still there is no relief! Yes, we should be taking advantage of whatever remedy we find. It can only be us, though. I know I just suggested that other wizards join too, but it is dangerous, and we do not want that for our brethren. We shall protect and hide this site."

"How, then, will we get other wizards to join us in our fight? We are strong now, yes, but we need the backing of the order to flush out the worlox permanently," Drystom stated.

"That is an excellent point, and one we must handle with great care. How do we protect our knowledge while showing the wizards that we now have the edge that will finally bring victory? We can be honest only to a point. Our goal is not to endanger anyone else. We have made this commitment by our own volition. Therefore, let us approach this in a way that they can understand and that will benefit us all. Tell the magister and the council that we were each visited by a sala who granted us special abilities in leadership and power so that the worlox can at last be vanquished," said Lorkai.

"Do you think it will work?" asked Closna.

"It has to. I will make it work. We have a duty to Goandria to destroy the worlox, and with the other wizards behind us, we will be unstoppable!"

"What is the plan from here?" Drystom asked.

"We head back to the temples, tell them our 'story,' and announce a major push against the worlox. It is hard to say if their infighting has ceased or not, and if it hasn't, that means we have even more of an advantage because their forces will be divided. The rest of the wizards will either join us or stand in our way and hinder peace from blossoming. It is our duty now to right the wrongs of our ancestors." Then the general addressed the rest of the wizards. "This land is to be protected at all costs. No one outside of us shall know where it is. That includes our friends and our families. We shall take an oath to protect this geyser and to never speak of it to anyone else."

Lorkai and the others reached out their hands, and a transparent-red dome formed over the magical energy. More formed on top of that like layers in an onion. Lorkai bent down, picked up a rock and threw it at the dome layers. It completely disintegrated on contact of the magical barrier. The general flared his fingers as he reached out and closed his eyes. The domes and the geyser faded until they were no longer visible. "This shall hide it from both friend and foe. No one except us may access the geyser."

"We will have to make regular trips here to recharge our magic," a wizard said.

"Indeed, which is why I placed a key in the protection. The only way any of us can access this area again is with a drop of our own blood. Now, each of you prick your finger and reach your hand out. This will reveal the domes. Once that happens, place your hands upon it, and the barrier will be down. However, in doing so, you have committed to the oath, and the magic cast here will hold you to it."

The other seventeen wizards did as Lorkai instructed. They all made the oath with smiles on their faces and confidence in their hearts.

Chapter 9

"Evera, do you understand the seriousness of what you and Lorkai have done?" the magister asked as he paced in front of her. "Lorkai, I expect defiance from, but not you. Sneaking out of the temples to disobey a direct order is childish and unbecoming of a wizard. From what you told me, you do not even know if your mission was successful because Lorkai continued that on his own. That just makes the matter far worse. Insubordination has no place among us, and you would do well to remember that in the future."

"Do I still have a future here, sir?" When Evera asked the question, the wizard council members shifted uncomfortably in their seats.

"We spent a lot of time discussing that very topic, as you well know. It was hard for us to come to any sort of agreement. There are some present who believe you should be expelled, but there are others who think you are a valuable asset to the wizard order and should stay." The magister continued his pacing for a minute before halting to face Evera. His gray eyes bore unblinkingly into her. They felt cold, unfeeling, and unpredictable. "Since," the magister began, spraying a few droplets of saliva onto Evera's face, "the council was divided on the matter, it came down to my decision after listening to what my colleagues had to say."

"And what was your decision?"

"You are to hand in your sword immediately, and you are suspended from all usage of your wizard powers or any activity that you would engage in specifically as a wizard for one week. After your suspension period, you are free to return to your job as a scholar."

Evera exhaled, realizing she had been holding her breath. "Oh, thank you!" She beamed, shaking the magister's hand.

"Any more direct disobedience to an order the council or I give will be met with a swift expulsion from the wizard order," the magister replied, reaching out his hand, palm up. Evera unbuckled her sword belt and handed it over.

"Now, to a less dreary topic. Tell me about this man you brought before us."

"I would not say it is particularly less dreary, magister. This man has been selling worlox ash to the village of Grivear, and possibly elsewhere. He admitted his crime to me and did come quietly when I confronted him on this issue."

"Is that so? Hmm." The magister resumed his pacing. "You find out that this man was selling worlox ash, but you don't know to how many or the precise damage it has caused, correct?"

"Yes," Evera said, narrowing one eye a bit.

"And you felt the need to bring him here because?"

Evera was dumbfounded. She searched for the right response, but her mind went blank. What should she tell him exactly? Was he testing her? What sort of answer was he even looking for? These were all questions that ran through her mind, but she did not know how to move forward in the conversation. She thought the answer to his question was obvious. This man broke the law, and now he must deal with the consequences of his actions.

"Evera?" he asked again.

"I, uh, wanted to stop him before the problem could spread any further. He was selling an illegal substance, and we saw first-hand what it did to two of his customers, one of which Lorkai had to kill because she attacked us with a sort of sorcery that manifested from her usage of the ash."

"That is troubling news indeed, but I fail to understand the need to bring him here."

"What exactly don't you understand? This man was ruining lives, magister, and his actions cannot be left unpunished."

"That is true, but you see, Evera, we are in a war. Our forces and resources are spread thin. Perhaps other magisters at other temples would have been intrigued with your discovery, but at this temple, our focus is the warfront. Most of the wizard army is stationed there, and the worlox are our priority, not some common criminal. Aside from all that, you have yet to offer any proof other than his confession. Did it occur to you that he confessed merely because you are a wizard?"

"Are you serious? This man was selling worlox ash. It has the potential to give limited magical abilities to people who are not subject to the boundaries and laws of the wizard order," Evera protested.

"I understand that, and I did not say I didn't believe you, just that we have very little to go on. Evera, I have been the magister for nearly ten years now, and I know when information is withheld. All I am saying is that based solely on the information you have presented to me, no further action is necessary beyond keeping him in our dungeons for two weeks. After two weeks, he will be free to go, and no more investigation is required into this matter."

"Sir, if I may…"

The magister lifted his hand to silence Evera. "No, you may not. Remember, you have been shown mercy, and it would be unwise to press your luck any further. We cannot root out this problem entirely. The wizards have a bigger picture to focus on."

"That is the problem in the first place! The ladies who used the ash and Rolaph all believe that the wizard order has abandoned them so they can fight this war. I can't help but agree with them. We are so focused on fighting this war that we have forgotten our main role in Goandria. Voshnore created the wizard order to protect and help the people whenever we can."

"That was before the worlox, Evera, before the demons crawled out of their holes and attempted to annihilate all living beings in Goandria. What we are doing *is* protecting the people of Goandria. The populations are finally beginning to come back after the initial worlox attack all those generations ago. People know that the worlox have lost the southern territories due to our efforts," countered the magister.

"Our job is also to feed the poor whenever we can and help the everyday people succeed when possible. Of course we cannot eradicate all problems of the world, but that does not mean we should wash our hands of it either. You were right to point out that there is a bigger picture. The bigger picture is the people who have become so neglected by us that they turn to less desirable things to help them."

"That is your perspective on this matter and yours alone. This council and I have no more to discuss on this matter."

"Really, that's it? You refuse to listen to any perspective outside of your own?"

"Your voice has been heard here, and this meeting is over. Good day, Evera."

"Unbelievable!" Evera shouted, storming out of the room.

Almost a week and a half passed before she was summoned to receive her sword back. Upon seeing the older man again, her face flushed and her pulse quickened. *They said a week! It has been longer than a week. They must think I have not noticed. Or perhaps the magister wanted to wait a little longer because of how I spoke to him. At least now I can return to my scrolls and hope they do not bother me with any more than assignments*, she thought as she approached the magister. Evera forced a smile as she shook his hand. *Ugh, look at him. So arrogant and self-righteous in his mission. Thinking he has this war under control when, in fact, everything is slipping through his fingers.*

"I trust you have learned a lesson here, Evera. Further insubordination will not be tolerated," the magister said, placing the weapon in Evera's hand.

"Yes, sir," she said meekly, forcing another smile.

Just then a young wizard abruptly burst into the room. "Magister! You had better come see this!" he said, half winded.

"What is it?"

"Just come. It would be better if you saw it for yourself, sir." The wizard led his master to a viewing area.

"Lorkai…" mouthed the magister.

Chapter 10

Lorkai and the other wizards approached the blessed temples with straight backs and proud chests. Each one marched in formation, their eyes unwavering, their right hands upon their belts, and their left hand at their sides. This signaled to those in the temples that they were leaders. All of them looked taller and stronger, exuding power from their very being and radiating an exotic air about them. Except for Lorkai, the wizards' eyes faintly glowed in the dim morning light, adding to their exquisiteness.

The wizards began to ascend the stairs to the temple. As Lorkai's boots touched the first step, leading the group, the temple gates swung open. The magister appeared at the top, surrounded by several other wizards. Their mouths dropped and their feet stopped moving as they recognized their comrades and noted the power they commanded. Some wondered how wizards who had just been freed from captivity could look so glorious.

"Lorkai, this is an unexpected pleasure. I see you were successful after all," announced the magister.

"Indeed I was, no thanks to you and the council." Lorkai glowered.

"Kai!" a woman's voice called out. Evera pushed her way past the other wizards and leapt into her friend's arms. "You made it! You are alive! I was so worried about you."

"I am fine~~okay~~, Evera," he said in monotone ~~without even looking at her~~ looking away.

"Kai?" her soft voice prodded to get his attention, but his gaze bore into the magister, and his upper lip had a slight curl in it. "What is it? Lorkai…" Ignoring her, Lorkai moved Evera to the side and unsheathed his sword.

"You!" Lorkai snarled as he approached the magister. "You were going to let them rot in the worlox dungeon. You and the sanctimonious council wanted to send me on some suicide mission when, in fact, these wizards hold the key to victory over the worlox."

"Lorkai, let's talk about this inside like civilized men."

"No, no more talking with you. We each were visited by a sala of Voshnore, and we were bestowed with powers beyond any wizard. You are now relieved of your command over these temples, as well as the council and any other magister that shares your narrow-minded perspective."

"You cannot order me about! You may be the general, but you…" the magister began, but with a snap of Lorkai's fingers, his voice was quickly silenced, though his lips kept moving. Turning to the other wizards who stood watch, Lorkai said, "Let it be known, you must join us or stay out of our way. The wizard order will no longer be more concerned with politics than the war. The time has come to eradicate the worlox. Any who share that vision will take part in Voshnore's greater plan for us all. He has sent his messengers to bless us with special abilities to destroy our enemies."

Evera watched her friend as he made his grandiose claims. Tears rolled down her cheeks, and her chest tightened. She could not believe what she was seeing.

"Lorkai!" she screamed, finally gaining his attention. Pulling him aside, she mumbled, "What has gotten into you? You cannot just take over like this."

"Evera, I'm doing what is best."

"You're different," she breathed, taking a step back. "What happened since we parted?"

"Evera, now is not the time for this."

"Yes! It is the time. You are my friend, and I care about you. Something is wrong with you. I can see it in your eyes. You are cold. You don't even seem happy to see me."

"Evera…"

"Don't! I don't want excuses or procrastinations. I want the truth. After you freed them, you went to the geyser, didn't you?"

"Yes, I did."

"Oh, Lorkai, you need to stop now."

Lorkai's nostrils flared. "You would stand in my way? I have found a way to win. We do not need to have more generations fighting the worlox."

"You told the magister it was from Voshnore, but the geyser you told me about probably has a connection to the worlox."

"Shh!" Lorkai snapped.

"You are lying to your own people!"

"It is for their own good, Evera. The wizards must be ruled with order and strength, not the cowardice of men like the magister and the council. Now, you either join me or stay out of my way, but if you try to reveal my secret to anyone, I will treat you like an enemy." With that, Lorkai turned to Drystom. "Bind the magister. Then lead the others to find the council, and do the same to them as well. It is time our brothers and sisters know that a new dawn is at hand and the council and magister no longer have any power." Lorkai marched off, leaving Evera speechless.

Word quickly spread of Lorkai's return, and when he called for an impromptu meeting in the dining hall, it was not long before every seat was filled. Evera elected to stand against the back wall, watching her friend and those who came back with him display the magister and the council as prisoners. The former rulers of the wizards were bound and gagged, tied to chairs, as the eighteen new leaders stood behind them. Once it appeared to Lorkai that everyone was present, he began walking back and forth behind his previous commander. "Thank you all for coming. As you all know, this has been a long, hard war for hundreds of years. All present, the young and the old, the scholar and the teacher, have been affected by the terrible atrocities afflicted upon us by the worlox. Humans, englifs, and ferrorians have all been enslaved and massacred by those demons."

As Lorkai began his speech, Evera noticed the odd, black, veiny streaks under his skin and the darker color of his eyes. *The worlox ash. It had to be. Or perhaps it was this new power you decided to play with. Either way, you are not the same man I knew. You changed and changed quickly. Oh, Lorkai, why did you have to mess with something you didn't understand?* she thought solemnly, trying to hold back tears as she listened to Lorkai.

"But no longer!" Lorkai continued. "We will not continue to lose husbands and wives, brothers and sisters, fathers and mothers, sons and daughters to those monsters. If we send the worlox back to where they came from, how do we know they will not return in the future? We don't! Therefore, the only solution is to eradicate them! We shall hunt them down like they have hunted us for so long. The sala, messengers of Voshnore himself, have visited each of us, bestowing a new kind of power on us so that we may carry out his will of destroying the demons. No one will be enslaved or oppressed by the worlox tyrants any longer!

"You may ask why I have the council and the magister of these temples tied up. To expose the truth! These men have withheld facts from you and refused to change their ways after not gaining any ground against the worlox. They have failed to listen to advice and pleas from their peers, and they set up an air of superiority about them. When I arrived here from the battlefield, I asked that they would allow me to save the fellow wizards standing beside me, but they refused my request. Instead, they wanted me to go on a suicide mission and *try* to send the worlox back to their home dimension. This plan was clearly put together to eliminate me. These men do not want us asking questions. They want utter obedience while they sit on a pile of secrets, but no more! We will use the gifts endowed by Voshnore to lead you to victory. Fight beside me, and the worlox will forever be eradicated! All who wish to join me will take part in making history, but any who stand in our way will be considered enemies."

Lorkai concluded, and the room erupted with applause. Evera stood aghast, tears streaking her red cheeks. "Lorkai, what have you done?"

Epilogue

In these dark times, I take it upon myself to document what has transpired of late. We are at a turning point in the world, and I pray what was unleashed can be contained. I write this in hopes that future generations will not make the same mistakes, that the wizard order may learn from the evils of my generation.

It is hard to believe that nearly twenty years have passed since Lorkai first led our order against the worlox. With new magic in his arsenal, he soon laid the worlox to waste. At the time, Lorkai led everyone to believe he had a divine mission from Voshnore and he was going to create a new era of peace for the future.

In the beginning, Lorkai was embraced. He seized leadership of our order, and the wizards marched alongside him into battle. The first thing Lorkai did with this power was throw all magisters and councils from all wizard temples throughout Goandria into dungeons. The once-great leaders of our order were reduced to starving in diseased and rat-infested prisons. But with the victories against the worlox, few seemed to even notice. Where decisions were once based on discussion and thought, they now hinged entirely upon Lorkai's will. The former leaders of our order were not the only ones to suffer such a fate. Everyone else whom the councils had imprisoned were never released, even when their sentence had passed. Lorkai saw them all as criminals and would often say he owed them nothing. Rolaph was one of those that never saw the light of day again. Rolaph had done terrible things, but he did not deserve to spend the rest of his life in prison. Perhaps when I met him, I would have thought differently, but his actions came out of desperation, not malevolence.

It was during our final push against the worlox that more infighting erupted within the worlox ranks. We never understood why. Perhaps they disagreed on the right way to handle Lorkai and our armies. It appeared that harmony was at last coming to Goandria. After hard-fought victories and the sight of families returning to Goandria, we thought the peace Lorkai promised was at hand.

I tearfully write that this was not the case. About that time, many wizards began to question Lorkai's methods and leadership. He slowly became tyrannical, making the wizards march with little food or rest. If anyone questioned his orders, they were imprisoned or worse. He eventually became paranoid, believing that people were plotting against him when they weren't. This was not the Lorkai I knew. This was not the man who was my closest friend and ally through the worlox war. His behavior caused a divide in the wizard order. Some followed Lorkai, but others chose to oppose him, for it did not take long before many wizards realized there was an evil behind Lorkai's new powers. Lorkai had not just changed, but he continued to change for the worse.

In merely five years, the worlox had been successfully eradicated. That did not stop Lorkai, though. He obsessively sought out enemies where none were to be found. After a few years of chasing ghosts, he simply disappeared. I thought his madness and the powers he was using had finally caught up to him. I mourned the loss of my friend. I cried for weeks, not just because he was lost, but because of how I lost him. He was once a kind man, a loving man, someone who would sacrifice anything for others, but perhaps his nature was his downfall. He tapped into a power that he did not understand, something wizards are forbidden to do, and it was at a great cost to him and all others who dared to do the same.

As I write, the world is again on the brink of collapse. Darkness is everywhere, and at the heart of this darkness is Lorkai, though he now calls himself Harkendor. The first schism in the history of the wizard order has occurred. Wizards loyal to Harkendor now fight against us, and the worlox have just been replaced by another monster, perhaps a greater monster. The wizard order is torn apart from civil war. I can't believe this was the Lorkai I knew. I cannot believe it. What a horrible and cruel fate for someone who fought so hard to free the people of Goandria. I do not know if the worlox ash he once was treated with has contributed to his fall, or if his own obsession with power and the use of prohibited magic is to blame.

I do not know what the future holds. I do not know if the wizards will even survive this storm. I pray that Voshnore delivers us from this evil and, if possible, restores Lorkai to the man he once was.

Coming late 2015

Goandria: Visions of War

Several generations after *The Schism*, Aron, a knight of the Republics, is betrayed as old enemies form new alliances against the people of Goandria. Look for this new, exciting novel soon!

Rivershore Books

www.rivershorebooks.com
blog.rivershorebooks.com
www.facebook.com/rivershore.books
www.twitter.com/rivershorebooks
Info@rivershorebooks.com

Made in the USA
Columbia, SC
06 October 2017